ANNE MO

CW00338152

MURDER ON FRE|

ANNE Morice, *née* Felicity Shaw, was born in Kent in 1916.

Her mother Muriel Rose was the natural daughter of Rebecca Gould and Charles Morice. Muriel Rose married a Kentish doctor, and they had a daughter, Elizabeth. Muriel Rose's three later daughters—Angela, Felicity and Yvonne—were fathered by playwright Frederick Lonsdale.

Felicity's older sister Angela became an actress, married actor and theatrical agent Robin Fox, and produced England's Fox acting dynasty, including her sons Edward and James and grandchildren Laurence, Jack, Emilia and Freddie.

Felicity went to work in the office of the GPO Film Unit. There Felicity met and married documentarian Alexander Shaw. They had three children and lived in various countries.

Felicity wrote two well-received novels in the 1950's, but did not publish again until successfully launching her Tessa Crichton mystery series in 1970, buying a house in Hambleden, near Henley-on-Thames, on the proceeds. Her last novel was published a year after her death at the age of seventy-three on May 18th, 1989.

BY ANNE MORICE
and available from Dean Street Press

ANNE MORICE

MURDER ON FRENCH LEAVE

With an introduction and afterword by
Curtis Evans

DEAN STREET PRESS

Published by Dean Street Press 2021

Copyright © 1972 Anne Morice

Introduction & Afterword © 2021 Curtis Evans

All Rights Reserved

First published in 1972 by Macmillan

Cover by DSP

The publisher thanks Mike Morris for providing essential material to
this publication

ISBN 978 1 913527 97 6

www.deanstreetpress.co.uk

INTRODUCTION

BY 1970 the Golden Age of detective fiction, which had dawned in splendor a half-century earlier in 1920, seemingly had sunk into shadow like the sun at eventide. There were still a few old bodies from those early, glittering days who practiced the fine art of finely clued murder, to be sure, but in most cases the hands of those murderously talented individuals were growing increasingly infirm. Queen of Crime Agatha Christie, now eighty years old, retained her bestselling status around the world, but surely no one could have deluded herself into thinking that the novel *Passenger to Frankfurt*, the author's 1970 "Christie for Christmas" (which publishers for want of a better word dubbed "an Extravaganza") was prime Christie—or, indeed, anything remotely close to it. Similarly, two other old crime masters, Americans John Dickson Carr and Ellery Queen (comparative striplings in their sixties), both published detective novels that year, but both books were notably weak efforts on their parts. Agatha Christie's American counterpart in terms of work productivity and worldwide sales, Erle Stanley Gardner, creator of Perry Mason, published nothing at all that year, having passed away in March at the age of eighty. Admittedly such old-timers as Rex Stout, Ngaio Marsh, Michael Innes and Gladys Mitchell were still playing the game with some of their old élan, but in truth their glory days had fallen behind them as well. Others, like Margery Allingham and John Street, had died within the last few years or, like Anthony Gilbert, Nicholas Blake, Leo Bruce and Christopher Bush, soon would expire or become debilitated. Decidedly in 1970—a year which saw the trials of the Manson family and the Chicago Seven, assorted bombings, kidnappings and plane hijackings by such terroristic entities as the Weathermen, the Red Army, the PLO and the FLQ, the American invasion of Cambodia and the Kent State shootings and the drug overdose deaths of Jimi Hendrix and Janis Joplin—leisure readers now more than ever stood in need of the intelligent escapism which classic crime fiction provided. Yet the old order in crime fiction, like that in world politics and society, seemed irrevocably to be washing away in a bloody tide of violent anarchy and all round uncouthness.

Or was it? Old values have a way of persisting. Even as the generation which produced the glorious detective fiction of the Golden Age finally began exiting the crime scene, a new generation of younger puzzle adepts had arisen, not to take the esteemed places of their elders, but to contribute their own worthy efforts to the rarefied field of fair play murder. Among these writers were P.D. James, Ruth Rendell, Emma Lathen, Patricia Moyes, H.R.F. Keating, Catherine Aird, Joyce Porter, Margaret Yorke, Elizabeth Lemarchand, Reginald Hill, Peter Lovesey and the author whom you are perusing now, Anne Morice (1916-1989). Morice, who like Yorke, Lovesey and Hill debuted as a mystery writer in 1970, was lavishly welcomed by critics in the United Kingdom (she was not published in the United States until 1974) upon the publication of her first mystery, *Death in the Grand Manor*, which suggestively and anachronistically was subtitled not an "extravaganza," but a novel of detection. Fittingly the book was lauded by no less than seemingly permanently retired Golden Age stalwarts Edmund Crispin and Francis Iles (aka Anthony Berkeley Cox). Crispin deemed Morice's debut puzzler "a charming whodunit . . . full of unforced buoyancy" and prescribed it as a "remedy for existentialist gloom," while Iles, who would pass away at the age of seventy-seven less than six months after penning his review, found the novel a "most attractive lightweight," adding enthusiastically: "[E]ntertainingly written, it provides a modern version of the classical type of detective story. I was much taken with the cheerful young narrator . . . and I think most readers will feel the same way. Warmly recommended." Similarly, Maurice Richardson, who, although not a crime writer, had reviewed crime fiction for decades at the *London Observer*, lavished praise upon Morice's maiden mystery: "Entrancingly fresh and lively whodunit. . . . Excellent dialogue. . . . Much superior to the average effort to lighten the detective story."

With such a critical sendoff, it is no surprise that Anne Morice's crime fiction took flight on the wings of its bracing mirth. Over the next two decades twenty-five Anne Morice mysteries were published (the last of them post-humously), at the rate of one or two year. Twenty-three of these concerned the investigations of Tessa Crichton, a charming young actress who always manages to cross paths with murder, while two, written at the end of her career, detail cases of Detective Superintendent "Tubby" Wiseman. In 1976 Morice along with Margaret Yorke was chosen to become a member of Britain's prestigious Detection Club, preceding Ruth Rendell by a year, while in the 1980s her books were included in Bantam's superlative paperback "Murder Most British" series, which included luminaries from both present and past like Rendell, Yorke, Margery Allingham, Patricia Wentworth, Christianna Brand, Elizabeth Ferrars, Catherine Aird, Margaret Erskine, Marian Babson, Dorothy Simpson, June Thomson and last, but most certainly not least, the Queen of Crime herself, Agatha Christie. In 1974, when Morice's fifth Tessa Crichton detective novel, *Death of a Dutiful Daughter*, was picked up in the United States, the author's work again was received with acclaim, with reviewers emphasizing the author's cozy traditionalism (though the term "cozy" had not then come into common use in reference to traditional English and American mysteries). In his notice of Morice's *Death of a Wedding Guest* (1976), "Newgate Callendar" (aka classical music critic Harold C. Schoenberg), Seventies crime fiction reviewer for the *New York Times Book Review*, observed that "Morice is a traditionalist, and she has no surprises [in terms of subject matter] in her latest book. What she does have, as always, is a bright and amusing style . . . [and] a general air of sophisticated writing." Perhaps a couple of reviews from Middle America—where intense Anglophilia, the dogmatic pronouncements of Raymond Chandler and Edmund Wilson notwithstanding, still ran rampant among mystery readers—best indicate the cozy criminal appeal of Anne Morice:

> Anne Morice . . . acquired me as a fan when I read her "Death and the Dutiful Daughter." In this new novel, she did not disappoint me. The same appealing female detective, Tessa Crichton, solves the mysteries on her own, which is surprising in view of the fact that Tessa is actually not a detective, but a film actress. Tessa just seems to be at places where a murder occurs, and at the most unlikely places at that . . . this time at a garden fete on the estate of a millionaire tycoon. . . . The plot is well constructed; I must confess that I, like the police, had my suspect all picked out too. I was "dead" wrong (if you will excuse the expression) because my suspect was also murdered before not too many pages turned. . . . This is not a blood-curdling, chilling mystery; it is amusing and light, but Miss Morice writes in a

polished and intelligent manner, providing pleasure and entertainment. (Rose Levine Isaacson, review of *Death of a Heavenly Twin, Jackson Mississippi Clarion-Ledger*, 18 August 1974)

I like English mysteries because the victims are always rotten people who deserve to die. Anne Morice, like Ngaio Marsh et al., writes tongue in cheek but with great care. It is always a joy to read English at its glorious best. (Sally Edwards, "Ever-So British, This Tale," review of *Killing with Kindness*, *Charlotte North Carolina Observer*, 10 April 1975)

While it is true that Anne Morice's mysteries most frequently take place at country villages and estates, surely the quintessence of modern cozy mystery settings, there is a pleasing tartness to Tessa's narration and the brittle, epigrammatic dialogue which reminds me of the Golden Age Crime Queens (particularly Ngaio Marsh) and, to part from mystery for a moment, English playwright Noel Coward. Morice's books may be cozy but they most certainly are not cloying, nor are the sentiments which the characters express invariably "traditional." The author avoids any traces of soppiness or sentimentality and has a knack for clever turns of phrase which is characteristic of the bright young things of the Twenties and Thirties, the decades of her own youth. "Sackcloth and ashes would have been overdressing for the mood I had sunk into by then," Tessa reflects at one point in the novel *Death in the Grand Manor*. Never fear, however: nothing, not even the odd murder or two, keeps Tessa down in the dumps for long; and invariably she finds herself back on the trail of murder most foul, to the consternation of her handsome, debonair husband, Inspector Robin Price of Scotland Yard (whom she meets in the first novel in the series and has married by the second), and the exasperation of her amusingly eccentric and indolent playwright cousin, Toby Crichton, both of whom feature in almost all of the Tessa Crichton novels. Murder may not lastingly mar Tessa's equanimity, but she certainly takes her detection seriously.

Three decades now having passed since Anne Morice's crime novels were in print, fans of British mystery in both its classic and cozy forms should derive much pleasure in discovering (or rediscovering) her work in these new Dean Street Press editions and thereby passing time once again in that pleasant fictional English world where death affords us not emotional disturbance and distress but enjoyable and intelligent diversion.

Curtis Evans

PROLOGUE

'WELL, who's going to get murdered on this trip, I wonder?' my cousin Ellen asked, studying our reflections in the mirror as I replaced my ticket, passport and travellers' cheques neatly in my bag and then tipped them all back on the formica shelf to unearth the small-change purse.

'You are,' I informed her, 'if there's any more of that talk. This is strictly a holiday, so far as Robin is concerned, with no nasty crime to spoil things, so try to remember that. I should remind you that you are here on sufferance as it is, and if word gets around the French capital that we are travelling with the fameux Inspecteur du Scotland Yard, I shall know who's responsible. You'll find yourself on the next plane back to that domestic science outfit.'

'I should think I've been expelled by this time,' she replied calmly.

'They can sort that out when you get there,' I told her, finding an English coin at last among all the francs and depositing it in the saucer.

I did not catch her riposte to this, because it was smothered by the public address system announcing a delay of twenty minutes in the departure of Air France Flight Eight Two Nine to Orly, owing to the late arrival of the incoming aircraft.

'So you will have time for the duty-free shop, after all, Tessa,' she said philosophically. 'That should help to get Robin's holiday off on the right foot.'

ONE

(i)

'WHAT should I buy?' Ellen asked, as we edged our way through the noisy, overheated departure lounge towards the duty-free supermarket. 'Brandy? Vodka?'

'No, you're under age and Robin is not on holiday to that extent. You might go and find him and explain what's happened. He may not have heard the announcement. They don't tell us what caused the delay to the incoming aircraft, you notice?'

'I expect it took them longer than usual to find the bombs. Anyway, Robin's not worried; he's teamed up with the great dane. They're over by the window.'

I glanced towards it and easily picked out the back of Robin's blond head, but the farouche-looking man facing him was a stranger to me and I felt positive that, once seen, I could never have forgotten him. He was wearing a bulky, greenish overcoat, open to reveal a brown tweed jacket, with a maroon pullover under that, and there was something self-consciously exhibitionist about him, even at a distance. It was not merely the impression he gave of having flung on whatever garments first came to hand which distinguished him from the average traveller; there was also a defiance in his thrust-up chin and roving glance, hinting that he was supremely indifferent to what others thought of the result, so long as they thought something. If I had been playing the personality game, though, I would not have given him the dog image. He looked to me more like some untidy old bird, and one could picture him whirling down corridors, the overcoat flapping behind and beak thrust forward, about to stake out a stiffish claim for his territorial rights.

'Why did you call him a great dane?' I asked, as we formed up in the queue for the cash register.

'Well, he's either that, or a train robber with forged papers. I saw his passport. He was standing just behind us when you checked in. I think his nerves got all in a jangle over the time you took writing a cheque for the excess baggage. That red suitcase was the last straw. What have you got in it, apart from bombs?'

'Apart from those, just my shoes and all those scripts my agent unloaded on me at the last minute. And my jewellery, come to think of it. Oh damn!'

'What now?'

'Something I forgot. Can't be helped, though.'

'Well, anyway, this man was getting in a fantastic stew and waving his passport around and I saw it was a Danish one.'

'He's certainly not speaking Danish, to judge by the fascinated expression on the back of Robin's head. Oh, is it my turn now? How lovely!'

As we emerged into the lounge again there was a second announcement on the public address system, regretting the further delay to Flight Eight Two Nine to Paris.

'More bombs,' Ellen said resignedly. 'Oh look! Robin's friend has gone. I expect he's given up.'

'Not gone for good,' Robin said when we joined him, 'Only as far as the bar. He's buying me a drink.'

'He might have waited for us,' I complained, slinging my bag and bottles on to the green leather chair, where Robin had already disposed half a dozen pieces of hand luggage and a couple of extra coats. 'A drink is what I feel I could do with. Since we seem destined to remain in this doom-laden place for the entire weekend, we might as well enjoy ourselves.'

'I shan't enjoy myself if you start drinking at four-thirty in the afternoon,' he told me. 'We've got enough complications without your lurching on to the plane minus your ticket and passport.'

'I hope I don't count as a complication,' Ellen said sadly. 'Though I suppose I must do, when you think of it. I shall cheer myself up with a coke. How about you, Tessa?'

'A coke would be better than nothing,' I agreed. 'I'll take two of my seasick pills and get high that way.'

'Is he a film director?' I asked, when Ellen had gone.

'Who?'

'Your kind friend, who's buying you a drink.'

'No, try again.'

'Script writer?'

'No, you're stuck in the wrong groove. It's all that show-off which reminds you of your own profession. This one works for IDEAS.'

'How quaint! I usually prefer to make them work for me.'

'I.D.E.A.S. It's an offshoot of United Nations. International Division for Engineering and Science. Their head . . .'

'Tell me later,' I mumbled, 'he's coming back.'

'Thank you very much,' Robin said smugly, as he accepted his treble pink gin. 'This is my wife, by the way.'

'Carlsen,' the man said, bringing his heels together and pulling my hand up to the regulation two inches from his nose.

'She was convinced that you had some connection with the film business.'

'Coming from you, madame, I take that as a tremendous compliment.'

'But Robin tells me you're with something called IDEAS. It sounds rather mysterious.'

'Oh no, all too prosaic, I'm afraid. Do let me get you a drink?'

'You're very kind, but my cousin is getting me one.'

'That rather smashing young person I saw you with just now? Asinine of me, but I took her for your sister.'

'Oh well, she's eight years younger than me, but she could be my sister, I suppose; if I had one.'

'And is she going on the stage?'

'It's odd you should say that,' I replied, 'because that is exactly her intention.'

'With those looks, it was an easy guess.'

'Unfortunately, her father does not see it in quite the same light. That is partly why she is coming to Paris with us.'

'Aha! So you are abducting her, I take it?'

'It might be truer to say that she is abducting us,' Robin remarked.

'Here you are, Tessa!' the abductress said, joining us at this point. 'See how you care for that.'

'Delicious,' I said, tasting it. It was, too, and I particularly liked the lacing of rum which she had been thoughtful enough to provide. 'I don't think I'll need the seasick pills, after all.'

'You're a bad traveller, Mrs Price?'

'It's not so much the travelling I mind. It's the bits in between.'

'Like this rotten delay. I do so agree. The maddening thing is that my wife's meeting me at Orly, and she's not going to be very pleased.'

'Can't you put a call through to warn her?'

'Unfortunately, it's too late for that. She's quite capable of driving at a hundred and fifty kilometres and she certainly knows all the short cuts and back doubles, but even so it will take her more than an hour to get to Orly from our side of Paris and she will have left already.'

'We have a car meeting us, too,' Robin said, 'but it's to be hoped that the driver is hardened to this kind of thing.' Privately I considered that Mrs Carlsen would have done better to stay over on her side of Paris, warming the slippers, but this prejudice probably arose mainly from the vaguely liverish kind of ill-humour which often accompanies long waits at airports and, luckily, I had not drunk enough Coca-Cola to give expression to it.

'And is yours a purely pleasure trip, Mrs Price? How long will you stay?'

'Robin is only coming for a few days. I have to spend six weeks, at least. Ellen's future is still in the balance.'

'Six weeks? That's quite a long holiday.'

'No holiday, I assure you. On Wednesday I start work.'

'Really? May I be terribly impertinent and ask what kind of work? Something to do with the haute couture, one would hazard a guess.'

Hazard was the word and I stared at him, momentarily speechless. It was not that I expected to be recognised by strangers. I was accustomed to passing unnoticed in the thinnest of crowds, or, at best, receiving the stony stare which indicates that someone knows the face but can't put a name to it. Nevertheless, by some process which now seemed shamefully conceited, I had arrived at the belief that Mr Carlsen had recognised me from the start and had known exactly how I earned my living.

'Tessa's an actress,' Robin explained. 'She is going to France to make a film.'

Rather more puzzlement must have shown on my face than I could have wished, for Mr Carlsen leant forward and said in his eager way:

'Oh, I say, what an appalling boob! Do forgive me for being such a clot. Of course I know now . . .'

'There's nothing whatever to forgive,' I said irritably. 'It's simply that I feel scared to death by the whole set-up and if no one in France is even going to believe I'm an actress it will be worse than ever.'

'Oh, but they will, I promise you. I felt certain I'd seen your face before and I remember perfectly now. Marvellous film about two years ago . . . what was it called . . . ? You were terrific, I do remember that. I say, if it wouldn't sound like fearful cheek, do tell me the name of your studios. As it happens, I have one or two chums in that world, and if it would help to oil the wheels for you I should be only too delighted . . .'

One way and another, he was piling it on far too thickly and it was mainly impatience with these clumsy attempts to make amends which drove me to the direct lie.

'I'm afraid I can't remember. It's all written down somewhere in my luggage, but my mind's a complete blank at the moment.'

'Still, if you could tell me the name of your hotel?'

'We haven't got one. They've rented a flat for us. Unfortunately I can't remember the address of that, either.'

I flashed a warning look at Robin, but for once he was out of step and fished for his diary. I tried to kick him under the table, but Ellen was between us and it was she who let out the startled yelp. Miraculously, the female on the public address system intervened in the nick of time. She lifted her microphone and ordered us to proceed to gate number ten for immediate embarkation.

She gave this command in the peremptory tones of one who had had her eye on the Eight Two Nine passengers throughout the class and was in no mood to brook any more of their sloppy behaviour. I sprang up and laid feverish hands on the luggage.

'Come on, come on!' I said, doling out packages and coats. 'Not a moment to lose. Let's go before she changes her mind.'

'What was all that hysteria about?' Robin asked, as we shuffled docilely through gate number ten, 'It's not like you to get tetchy because someone doesn't rush up and plead for your autograph.'

'Not tetchy at all,' I muttered, 'what a fantastic suggestion! I just got the feeling he was trying to edge in a bit too fast. After all, we don't necessarily want him round our necks the whole time we're in Paris, do we?'

'No, and I shouldn't think there's the slightest danger of it. I imagine he was only trying to be helpful, and our paths are not likely to cross again.'

'I expect you're right,' I admitted. 'I didn't exactly fall for him, but nobody is at their best in a situation like that, and as you say we've probably seen the last of him.'

As I spoke, someone in the queue behind us lurched forward and caught me a stinging blow on the leg with his brief-case. I stumbled sideways and one of the extra coats, which I had draped over my shoulders, slithered to the ground. Ellen and I dived for it simultaneously, I got another buffeting with the brief-case, and its owner, bending down to retrieve the coat, knocked heads with Ellen, who promptly clasped her forehead and allowed the duty-free packages to tumble out on the ground. Robin, who already held a share of the small luggage in each hand, wisely kept aloof from the maelstrom, but, tearing up from behind like some intrepid outside left, Mr Carlsen joined in with a flying tackle.

'Oh, thank you, thank you. How kind! Thank you so much,' I repeated about fifty times, as he nimbly gathered up our possessions and placed them in our hands.

'Not at all, not at all, not at awl,' he countered, 'absolutely no trouble. Are you sure you can manage all these?'

'Yes, thanks awfully. We haven't far to go now.'

'Well, do have a marvellous and successful time in Paris, won't you?' he begged me earnestly. 'And I can't tell you how much I shall look forward to seeing the film. Any Theresa Crichton movie is an absolute "must" in our family.'

'There you are!' Robin said, as we stumbled through the last little tunnel of purgatory and on to the aircraft. 'He remembered your name, after all; and it only took him ten minutes. I expect you feel kindlier towards him now?'

But, oddly enough, I didn't.

(ii)

Mr Carlsen was travelling in what is genteelly called Economy Class, and the only reason for our not being in that category too was that the Company, on my agent's insistence, had issued me with a first-class ticket. I had been all for trading it in for a cheaper one and setting the profit against Robin's, but he would not hear of it. It was useless to point out that the Company had no interest whatever in the means by which I travelled to Paris, and provided I turned up at the studios at eleven o'clock on Wednesday morning I could crawl there on my hands and knees, for all they cared. He has a very strict moral code and the idea of getting something for nothing, or even part of something for nothing, was not to be entertained.

The last-minute inclusion of Ellen in the entourage had presented no financial problems, because her father and sole guardian, who is my cousin Toby Crichton, was passing through one of his affluent periods. I use the word 'passing' advisedly, because none of us expected much of the affluence to stick and Ellen and I, who do not have quite such a high moral code as Robin, had decided that some of it might just as well be dissipated on a jaunt to Paris as any other extravagance.

The reason for this aforementioned affluence, and also in a roundabout way for Ellen's presence, was that Toby was in New York, supervising rehearsals of his latest play, which was about to open on Broadway after a moderately successful London run. He had not wanted to go, pretending to loathe America and certainly loathing all forms of travel with no pretence at all, but the flattery of being invited to do so, plus some rather frigid correspondence with the Department of Inland Revenue, had temporarily got through his defences. Accustomed as he was to being ground into the dust by London producers, whose only concern with an author, once he has handed over the script, is that he should disappear and write another one, or, better still, drop dead, there had been something too heady to be resisted in the prospect of being paid to sit in on rehearsals and have some say in the style in which the actors should deliver his immortal lines.

Inevitably, the reaction had set in, even before American know-how went into action, and he found himself being bombarded by incomprehensible cables and awakened at four in the morning to engage in even less comprehensible telephone conversations; but by then his agent, who is also mine, had tied him up to the point of no return.

He had tried every dodge in his repertoire to loosen the chains which bound him, but, ironically enough, it was not until after he had been spooned on to the transatlantic liner that a valid excuse for staying at home had turned up, and Ellen had been the one to provide it.

She had used the occasion of her sixteenth birthday, some months previously, to declare her intention of abandoning the unequal struggle for O-levels in favour of going on the stage. There was nothing specially noteworthy about this, for I am reliably informed that approximately half a million sixteen-year-old girls all over the country were saying exactly the same thing at that very minute. The authorities, however, were ready for them. With masterly teamwork, they decreed that no one who had not already worked in the theatre for a minimum of forty weeks could obtain a union ticket, and no one under the age of eighteen could enrol at a reputable drama school. Even without benefit of O-levels Ellen could measure the cleft in this particular stick, and she had reluctantly settled for spending the first two years of her theatrical career resting, which Toby agreed was not a bad apprenticeship, in its way.

However, we had no sooner reached this tolerably satisfactory conclusion than some officious female acquaintance had to stick her oar in, by extolling the advantages of a domestic science course. The gleam which this lighted in Toby's eye was not to be extinguished by any arguments on our side, and it was easy to see why. If his only child were bent on entering a profession which offered little more than the prospect of perpetual unemployment, what more practical than to acquire a gracious, well-run home for himself while she was engaged in it?

In a spirit of deepest gloom, the wretched girl had been fitted out with overalls and secateurs and wooden spoons and, one week before Toby sailed for New York, had been turned loose on the Margaret Hacker Domestic Science College, two miles from Newbury. One week after he landed she had hitch-hiked the two miles to Newbury, boarded the London train and turned up on our doorstep.

It was my inevitable fate to be cast in the role of buffer state between Ellen and her father, for, standing midway between them in age, I provided a built-in, made-to-measure bridge for the generation gap. However, this particular crisis called for rather more delicate buffing than I had hitherto been called upon to supply, and the situation was aggravated by my own imminent departure for France. Possessing neither the inclination to return Ellen to Margaret Hacker, nor the right to do otherwise, I had pondered the matter for an hour or two and then despatched a chatty telegram to Toby, ending with the news that Ellen had run away.

'Where to love Toby,' he replied.

'Here of course love Tessa,' I cabled back; and heard no more.

No light had ever shone greener, as even Robin had to concede, and from a selfish point of view nothing could have fallen out better. Ellen was not only very gorgeous to look at, but apart from a slight mental block on the subject of O-levels and domestic science was amenable in all things and a constant pleasure to have around.

At this point in my remembrance of things past, she interrupted by saying:

'You forgot to unfasten your seat belt and now it's too late.'

'And you forgot to drink your free champagne, or don't you want it?'

'Not really. I'll swop it for your free sample of eau de toilette, if you like.'

We effected this small exchange and Robin handed over his free sample of after-shave lotion, which she said would come in handy for Toby's Christmas stocking. The wheels bumped on to the runway, reminding the air hostess to tell us what a pleasure it had all been and to mention in passing that the temperature outside was twenty-five degrees centigrade.

This was no sort of centigrade for trundling four extra coats and fourteen pieces of hand luggage along several miles of Orly airport, and we were the last bedraggled little flock to be herded into the immigration pen. Most of the passengers had already gone on their way by the time we reached the Customs Hall, and it was simple to pick out our luggage as it bumped lazily around on the moving bench. Ellen dived in to collect each piece as it came alongside and Robin coerced a porter into taking charge of it.

'C'est tout?' he demanded angrily, swinging his trolley towards the exit as each case was loaded on.

'Non, non,' Ellen cried, returning once more to the fray.

'I think that really is tout, isn't it?' Robin asked, after an unaccountable lull.

'Just one more to come.'

'Count them again,' he commanded a minute or two later. 'There can't be any more, they've battened down the hatches.'

'Then they must batten them up again. The red case hasn't come out yet and it's got my jewellery in it.'

'Sure you didn't leave it in the taxi?'

'Positive.'

'Was it locked?'

'It was when we left the house, but then I had to open it up again at Heathrow, to put those scripts in. I can't remember if I . . . Oh dear,' I said, clutching my head, 'perhaps champagne on top of Coca-Cola was a mistake, after all. I simply can't remember if I locked it again.'

'Well, you two had better wait here and I'll go and make some enquiries. There's probably a correct procedure for this kind of thing. I might even track down that chauffeur they've laid on for you. At least, I could prevent his giving a Gallic shrug and driving off without us.'

He spoke a few words to the customs official at the barrier and vanished into the free world.

'C'est tout?' the porter asked. 'On s'en va?'

I explained that we still awaited one valise the more, and proffered a ten-franc note towards compensation for his valuable time. He waved it away, muttering something whose full meaning escaped me and I had the uncomfortable feeling that it had not been nearly enough.

The three of us stared gloomily into space, alone on our desolate island in a sea of happy, carefree passengers cheerfully loading up their luggage from the neighbouring benches and making for the exit. One such group drove slap into Mr Carlsen, who came bursting through, overcoat flying and eyes frantically searching the hall.

'Good grief, what's this I hear?' he yelped, galloping towards us. 'I ran into the old man outside and he told me the ghastly news. Has the case turned up yet?'

'Not yet.'

'How desperately maddening for you! Now, look, if you wouldn't think it an unpardonable nerve, do give me an exact description, so that I can hand the problem over to a rather powerful chum of mine, who's more or less in charge here. That is, if you wouldn't think it the most beastly cheek?'

'No, it's very kind of you. I'm only surprised you're still around. We seem to have been languishing here for ages.'

'It was the sheerest fluke. Poor Adela was only allowed to park in the yard outside for half an hour, and when the plane was so late she had to move on. Now she has to walk about a mile to pick up the car again. She had just gone for it when your husband turned up. Really, this has been a most ill-fated journey, in many ways.'

'Yes, hasn't it? But, for goodness sake, don't be missing when your wife comes back. That would be the last straw.'

'Not to worry, your husband's standing guard over my shabby old luggage till she returns. She'll recognise it like a shot. Now, can you give me a description of the missing case, so that I can set some influential wheels in motion?'

'I'll write it down for you. And perhaps while I'm doing that you could pacify the porter? I'm afraid he's not pleased, but we intend to make it up to him.'

'Never fear, I'll soon sort him out. And don't forget to write down your address, will you? They can deliver the case to your flat, the minute it turns up.'

It was reasonable enough and he had spoken quite casually, and yet in the act of taking a pen from my bag the thought flashed through my head that the missing suitcase betokened something more sinister than just carelessness. I glanced up for another look at Mr Carlsen, but he had his back to me and was engaged in passionate conversation with the porter.

'Come over and help me, Ellen,' I called. 'You're much cleverer at this sort of thing than I am. What do you make of it?' I went on, dropping my voice. 'So many friends in so many high places, and it always ends with his asking for our address. One should guard against this Anglo-Saxon tendency to distrust all foreigners on principle, but I confess I'm finding it uphill work at the moment.'

'You think he might be a thief? Well, there's nothing much you can do about it,' she pointed out. 'If you play a trick of your own, like giving him a false address, you'll never get your case back.'

'That's true.'

'If you ask me, the big mistake was making all that secrecy about Robin's job.'

'You mean, if this man was a crook it would have scared him off? You may be right, but we can soon rectify that, you know. How's this: red crocodile dressing case. Gold initials T.P. Air France Flight Eight Two Nine from Heathrow. Please return to Detective Inspector Price, Eighth Floor, 201 avenue de Suffren, Paris 7.'

She nodded approvingly and I handed the page to Mr Carlsen, watching him through narrowed eyes as he skimmed through the message. But he was either a very cool, confident criminal, or a very innocent good Samaritan, for there were no flinches or guilty looks.

'Dandy!' he said. 'Couldn't be better, and I'll get moving on it right away. You'll probably have it back by tomorrow, at the latest. So your husband is in the police force, is he? I must ask him if he's ever come across an old buddy of mine, Roger McMahon, who used to work at the Yard.'

'I think most people there know him. He was Assistant Commissioner.'

'That's the one! Well, I think you can take your long-suffering porter away now, and I'll get busy. Fingers crossed!'

We found Robin waiting in the main hall, although there was no shabby luggage to identify him by.

'What's this?' I asked. 'Have we been duped, after all? Where's the female accomplice?'

'Mrs Carlsen? She came and went. Our driver carried the luggage out to their car. His name is Pierre, by the way, which is an easy one. He is now waiting for us outside, so if you haven't managed to dream up some fresh drama in the interval, perhaps we could be on our way?'

*

'What's she like?' I asked, as the car swept heedlessly into the terrors of the Auto-Route du Sud. 'Does she speak just as good English as her husband?'

'Almost. She's American.'

'Attractive?'

'Terrific.'

'Young?'

'I wouldn't have said so.'

'Then what would you say? You're being very cagey.'

'I know,' he said, sounding a trifle surprised all the same. 'And I can't explain it, but I didn't take to either of them madly. It's ungracious of me because she was radiant and he could hardly have been kinder. Perhaps that's at the bottom of it. People don't normally go so far out of their way to help perfect strangers.'

'You have put your finger on it,' I told him, 'and I am so relieved to be given a rational explanation for all my nasty prejudices and to know they're not just the aftermath of Coca-Cola.'

'I expect we do them an injustice, though. It's an occupational hazard to suspect innocent people of nameless crimes but we'll both feel much more charitable after a good night's sleep. And if the suitcase should turn up you can get their address from the telephone directory and send a polite note of thanks, to close the chapter. We must be nearly there, thank God! There's the Invalides.'

I ignored this historic landmark, however, for my attention had been caught by an elegant, galleon-shaped building away over to the right, which, unlike the Invalides, was ablaze with lights.

'What is it?' I asked.

'The IDEAS building,' Ellen replied, 'I've seen it on the postcards. And that's where Mr Carlsen works. What a coincidence! Just around the corner from our flat!'

(iii)

We were on the top floor of a shiny black apartment block, resembling a giant slab of liquorice, about two hundred yards from the Hilton Hotel.

It was too up-to-date to include a concierge among the amenities, which I regretted both for sentimental and practical reasons, and this feature had been replaced by rows of impersonal letter-boxes, with a door beside them labelled 'Bureau', although neither then nor at any time during our stay did we find anyone in occupation. Luckily, I had had the foresight to give Robin the keys and he needed every one of them, including two for the front door. This opened into a tiny hall and there were two bedrooms, with a bathroom leading out of the larger one, and a combined salon and dining-room. Every single room and cupboard was locked and so was the refrigerator. In view of this, it was rather disappointing to find that it was also empty.

Since it was past seven o'clock, Robin said he would take us out to dinner, provided we didn't expect the Hilton, and Ellen informed us that she had noticed plenty of shops still open, wherein to procure a few essentials for the morning. Robin handed her the bunch of keys, but she had already found a Judas peephole in the front door and said it would be much more fun to ring the bell, so that I could spy at her from within.

It was, too. From my side of the tiny glass disc, I had a clear view of the landing and part of the staircase, as well as of Ellen capering about and acting the part of a burglar.

Besides the morning's rations, which included several yards of loaf, she had acquired a very chic peaked cap in brilliant tartan, which I afterwards learnt she had bought for prix choc at the local supermarket. For the purposes of this charade, she had pulled it over her eyes and tied a handkerchief round the lower half of her face.

'Super miming,' I said, pulling open the door, as she raised her arm to cosh me with the loaf, 'and I can't wait to get one of these gadgets installed in our door in London.'

I referred to this again during dinner and Robin said:

'I thought we had agreed to keep off the subject of crime this weekend?'

'Oh, I wasn't thinking of criminals. I don't imagine that many burglars would dress themselves up like Ellen did and then ring the bell to be let in.'

'I expect Tessa thought it would be fun to spy on all your friends.'

'What a poisonous idea!'

'Useful, though. But still, let's not argue about that. I want to make some plans for tomorrow. Here we are in Paris, with four lovely, idle days ahead! How shall we spend them?'

'Nosing round the boutiques in Saint-Germain,' Ellen suggested.

'You can do that kind of thing just as well in London. I should have thought it might be more beneficial to nose round the Louvre, just for once. I want to go and see a lot of movies, too. I'm dead keen to polish up my French a bit, before I start work.'

'Well, here's the programme, then,' Robin said. 'You can both go shopping in the morning and I'll meet you for lunch and take you to the Louvre, or whatever, and we'll pack in a movie in the evening. That should satisfy all parties.'

'Particularly you,' I said, 'carving out a nice late morning in bed for yourself.'

'However, there's one little chore to be done first,' he told me.

'What's that?'

'To make a list of the jewellery in the red case and write to the insurance company. It may not be needed, but it wouldn't do to bank on it.'

'Altogether, it sounds an exhausting programme,' I sighed. 'At this rate, I shall be worn out before work even starts.'

Two

(i)

UNFORTUNATELY, events have a way of rearranging themselves to suit their own ends, even when Robin is in charge, and on Saturday morning his guiding hand was not even present. My base suspicions about his motives for sending us out shopping proved to be unfounded, for he was up and dressed and out of the flat before either of us had stirred.

'Tell me something, Ellen,' I said, as we drank our coffee and hacked our way through the loaf, which now had the substance of lead piping. 'Do you suppose they work on Saturdays at the Sûreté?'

'I should hope so. Don't they at Scotland Yard? And why do you want to know?'

'It's just that I was wondering what Robin could be up to. The only people he knows in Paris are policemen, and yet he was the one who was so keen to make this a real holiday, with no shop. Which reminds me that you and I had better get a move on, if we're going to get anything done this morning.'

The doorbell rang while I was in the bath, but Ellen was still on her own when I emerged a few minutes later. She was striking attitudes in front of my long mirror, and so far it hadn't cracked from side to side. Besides the peaked tartan cap, which was now on back to front, she was wearing jeans tucked into yellow suede boots, a Tibetan smock and a necklace made from dried beans.

'Very fetching,' I said.

'Do you think these jade ear-rings would be overdoing it a bit?'

'Oh, surely not? One would hardly notice them.'

'Unless there's another pair I could borrow in your red case? It's back, by the way.'

'No!'

'In the hall. I've just let it in.'

'How do you mean you let it in? Did it walk here on its own?'

'We may have been meant to think so. It didn't work out, actually.'

'Could you stop being cryptic, Ellen?'

'Well, I heard the lift come up, you see. When it gets as high as this floor, it must either be for us or the people next door, so I buzzed out to the spy-hole.'

'And?'

'And there was Mr Carlsen on the landing. He'd propped the lift door open with his brief-case and he plopped your red one down on the mat, rang the bell and nipped back into the lift again.'

'How extraordinary! There doesn't seem to be anything missing, though,' I said, turning over the contents one by one. 'So he's not a jewel thief, whatever else. Unless all these are glass copies, but I suppose even you would agree that he'd need to be a pretty fast operator to have got them made in the time? You realise what this means?'

'No, what?'

'I now have to tear up that carefully worded letter to the insurance company and begin carefully wording my note of thanks to Mr Carlsen. In the circumstances, it's going to be quite hard to phrase it.'

'Why not telephone?'

'That might get us even more involved. You know how weak-minded I am?'

As I spoke, the telephone rang and more involved is what we instantly became.

'Hallo! Mrs Price?'

'Yes, is that Mr Carlsen?'

'Clever you! I was wondering if you'd had any news of your suitcase?'

'The best. It's come back.'

'Gosh! That didn't take long, did it?'

'No, and thank you so much for all you've done. I gather you were entirely responsible.'

This put a finger in his dyke for a moment and during the ensuing pause I winked at Ellen. She had found another lovely French gadget, an extra earpiece clamped to the back of the telephone, and was making full use of it.

'One did one's tiny best,' Mr Carlsen said, rallying again, 'and there's nothing missing, I hope?'

'Not a thing. I'm really most grateful.'

'Don't mensh. I've only one teeny favour to ask in return.'

'Here we go!' I murmured, covering the mouthpiece. 'Oh yes?'

'I was wondering if I might have the pleasure of showing you around this little building of ours? It has some quite interesting features, if you happen to like modern architecture.'

'It's very kind of you; not the sort of favour I'm often asked for, I must say. The only snag is that I doubt if we'll have time. Robin has to leave on Tuesday and I start work the day after.'

'In that case, how about Monday morning? It doesn't take more than an hour to go round.'

'Well, I don't know . . . I'll have to ask Robin. He's not here at the moment, and he may have fixed something.'

'Well, do try to persuade him. And I hope you'll all have lunch with me afterwards. The restaurant isn't quite up to Grand Véfour standards, but they do you moderately well, with a fabulous view of Paris thrown in.'

'It sounds lovely, but the thing is we haven't got an awful lot of time.'

'Still you must eat. Come on, be a sport! Think of the thrill you'll be giving all those poor tired international workers!'

'You're very kind and we'll certainly do our best.'

'What else could I say?' I asked Ellen, as we both hung up. 'He appealed to my worse nature.'

'You could have said you were on a diet.'

'It wouldn't be true. Another breakfast like we've just had and I'll be ready to go anywhere for a square meal. Now let's concentrate for a moment and try to sort this out. Are we agreed that Mr Carlsen pinched the case, himself?'

'It looks like it.'

'But how? And how did he manage to conceal it about his person? It was too big to hide under his overcoat, and he certainly didn't have it with the rest of his luggage, otherwise Robin would have seen it.'

'All the same, there are a thousand ways it could have been worked.'

'Name them. Not all of them,' I added hastily, as she drew a deep breath, 'one good one will do.'

'I'll give you two. They're both good, but in one he's got Mrs as an accomplice and in the other he plays a lone hand.'

I considered this and then said: 'Yes, I suppose she could have taken it to their car before Robin arrived on the scene, but he wouldn't have had much time to make up a plausible excuse for having somebody else's luggage. Let's hear your other good one.'

'Okay, how's this? He knew that we were right at the back of the queue and had to keep stopping every five seconds to pick up something you'd dropped, so that gave him at least ten minutes to work in. So he picked up your red case and marched through the customs barrier. You remember how the man there was waving everyone through, so it was a million to one that he'd be asked to open it.'

'Then what?'

'Why, then he just nipped off to the consigne. All he had to do was shove it in a locker, pocket the key and go back to fetch it the next morning.'

'Yes, I'll accept that. It was rather clever of you to think of it, but it does mean that we're dealing with a raving lunatic. What possible reason could there be for doing such a thing? I thought at first that he was pestering us just to scrape acquaintance, but no sane person would go to such lengths as that. And consider the risk! If we had happened to catch him making off with the case, it would hardly have started the friendship on a very beautiful footing.'

'No, what I think is this, Tessa. It was the suitcase he was after all the time. I expect he heard you say it had your jewellery in it and he marked it down before we even left

Heathrow. Then he discovered Robin was a policeman and he got the wind up. But he'd done the deed by then, so the only hope was to undo it as quickly as possible.'

I had already noticed Ellen's predisposition for a criminal explanation wherever she could find one and was about to point out that an organisation such as IDEAS was unlikely to number professional thieves among its personnel, when the doorbell rang again.

'There's a sort of gypsy outside,' Ellen informed me, returning from her spy-hole. 'Shall I let her in?'

'Oh dear! Has she come to sell us something?'

'Could be. She's got a whopping great carrier bag with her.'

'Oh, let her in, then. I expect we could do with some clothes-pegs.'

She told us that her name was Lupe and, having shaken hands with great formality, strode off to the kitchen. She then removed her coat, shoes and watch, thrust them into the carrier bag, from which she had already taken an apron and some carpet slippers, and pitched into the washing-up with the enthusiasm of one who had been anticipating this particular treat all her life.

'I remember now,' I said, when we had jerked ourselves out of a stunned silence, 'There's a femme de ménage who goes with the flat. That's a break, isn't it? I imagine she's Spanish.'

My own Spanish was even weaker than my French, but Ellen had once spent a few months with me on location near Barcelona and she sped back to the kitchen for a brief refresher course, while I finished dressing.

'She's okay,' she informed me ten minutes later. 'She has four children and her sister has eight children. Or it could be the other way round. I'm not absolutely certain.'

'Don't worry,' I told her, 'it's not vital.'

'She also has a key to let herself in with. She didn't use it this morning because she was afraid of scaring you; or of you scaring her. I'm not sure which. They have this fantastic way of putting sentences back to front.'

'Never mind, you'll soon pick it up again. And just think what a linguist you're going to be. Lupe in the morning, French movies in the evening. It should do much to reconcile your father.'

'I know. I thought of that, too; but what I need most is some Paris clothes. Aren't you ready yet?'

'I'm so sorry, Ellen, but I honestly don't think I'll have time for it this morning. So many delays and we have to meet Robin at twelve. Why don't you go off on your own for a bit and join us at the café when you're through? You know where the Deux Magots is, or are?'

'Yah. It's that place just across from Le Drug Store,' she replied, making me feel my age.

(ii)

It was crowded, inside and out, with colourful left-bank characters, but not an English-type Detective Inspector in sight. It was a fine September morning and I took the last empty table on the pavement, the better to watch for his arrival. It was slightly disappointing to discover that half the vie de bohème around me was speaking English, but at least the pattern of behaviour was authentically foreign. The clientèle were nearly all young and most were in groups of eight or ten. Every two seconds one or other member of a group would bound to his feet, shake hands with everyone at the table and walk briskly away, in the manner of one who had just downed the last farewell drink before emigrating to Australia. Five minutes later, to the apparent surprise of no one, he would return, often with a fresh contingent of friends, for whom places were immediately found at the table. This was invariably the signal for another member of the group to jump up and repeat the entire performance. It reminded me of an elaborate game of postman's knock, or, come to that, of a second-rate film, where the director has nothing of significance to say but is determined to keep everyone on the move while he says it.

'Sorry I'm late,' Robin said, breaking in on these reflections. 'What's that you're drinking?'

'A Kyr. I can recommend it. In fact, I'm about ready for another, so you can ask the waiter for encore deux, if perchance you don't trust your pronunciation.'

'Oh, but I do. I trust it implicitly. I've been having a fascinating conversation with a most cultivated gentleman, and three-quarters of it in French. It's quite gone to my head.'

'So I see! What else happened at the Sûreté to create this euphoria?'

'Ah, you guessed, did you? Well, I wasn't making a mystery of it on purpose. I had to see an old buddy of mine who's attached to a branch of the Deuxième Bureau; la piscine, as we call it in the argot. He's been extremely cooperative on occasions and I felt it called for a courtesy visit. It might have caused offence if he discovered I'd been in Paris and not passed by his office to say Bonjour and so on. I wanted to get it done with and I literally expected it to take me ten or fifteen minutes. However.'

'However!'

'Well, we had a nice chat and it suddenly came into my head, just an impulse really, to ask if he knew anything about a certain Mr Sven Carlsen. It's ungrateful of me, I know, but I don't entirely trust that gentleman and I feel a bit curious about him. Any news of your suitcase, by the way?'

I brought him up to date on that situation, including the telephone call, and he said:

'There you are, Tessa! That's exactly the kind of thing I mean. What a crazy way to behave! Why go to all the trouble of driving out to the airport at crack of dawn for the sake of someone he'd only just met? We can't pretend he's a besotted fan because it was painfully obvious that he hadn't a clue who you were.'

I had a vague sensation of something off key in this remark, but did not mention it, lest Robin should attribute my protest to wounded vanity, and he went on:

'Presumably, you were meant to believe that some dim-witted messenger had dumped the case outside the front door, but why? Why not just have telephoned the good news and left it to the airline to deliver the case? It was entirely their responsibility, after all.'

'Well, Ellen and I have a theory about that, which I'll tell you in a moment, but something else has just struck me: how on earth did he find our telephone number? I'm positive I didn't write it down for him because I didn't know it myself, at that time.'

'It wouldn't have required much ingenuity, as it happens. You may not have noticed it, but those letter-boxes in the hall are arranged vertically, in pairs. Each pair has the floor number beside it and the name of the two tenants; the real tenants, that is, not itinerants like ourselves. So all he had to do was to look up two names in the telephone directory and he had an even chance of being right first go.'

'How clever of you to work that out! But you still haven't told me the real bit. What did you learn about him from your friend in the piscine?'

'Absolutely nothing. The old boy was awfully good and he got about fifty people sorting through the records, but not a thing turned up in any way connected with Carlsen. He was all set to extend the enquiries to the Danish police, but I thought that would be going too far, and I'm sure you agree.'

'Yes, I do, but since you've drawn such a mighty blank, what on earth are you looking so happy about?'

'Well, one thing led to another, you see, and that's what really kept me there so long. The fact that I'd mentioned IDEAS was the tiny item to draw him out on a matter which is giving certain people a big headache at the moment.'

'To do with IDEAS?'

'Possibly. What's happened is that, during the past four or five months, there have been some fairly serious leaks; on the espionage front, that is.'

'Oh lovely! Do tell me.'

'Well, It seems that none of the known agents have shown any special signs of activity lately, which is one reason why they thought it was time to take a fresh look at some of the international agencies. This is confidential, I might add, but I know you can be discreet, when necessary.'

'But what led them to suspect those people?'

'Past experience, presumably. They're all supposed to be loyal first and foremost to the United Nations and the concept of brotherhood of man, etcetera, and no doubt many of them do subscribe to those ideals and put national patriotism second; but one can hardly suppose there are no exceptions. Furthermore, I learnt an interesting fact about how the top-level people are recruited.'

'How?'

'Apart from the rare case where one man in the whole world is uniquely cut out for the job, the various member countries are invited to submit their own candidates. You can see what an unscrupulous government could do with a set-up like that?'

'Dust off their best spy, cook his curriculum vitae and tell him to land the job, or get ready to face the firing squad? I wonder they should bother, though. After all, there can't be much secrecy about their work. I should have thought it was all absolutely accessible to anyone who happened to possess an enquiring mind.'

'I wouldn't bank on that, but you've missed the point. It's not United Nations secrets which are being leaked. What you may not realise about IDEAS, for example, is that every post over a certain level automatically carries diplomatic privilege. They have those very distinctive green C.D. number-plates, for a start.'

'And can park anywhere they please, I suppose? How that would appeal to Toby! Perhaps we ought to try and fix a job for him here?'

'No, because it would mean living in France, and he would probably hate that even more than America. Besides, I was thinking of something a little more weighty than parking fines. What about a certain immunity from the ban on driving in and around those areas where the ordinary visitor is not welcomed?'

'You mean secret weapon factories and so on?'

'That kind of thing.'

'How fascinating! And do you mean that the boys in the piscine are going to ask you to stay on and give them a hand?'

'Good God, no. Whatever gave you that idea? I've simply been telling you this because I knew it would amuse you, and now you can have a lovely time weaving fantasies about

Sven Carlsen, the master spy. Apart from that, it doesn't concern us at all.'

'Oh, but Robin, I'm sure you could sort it all out for them in a trice, and just think how lovely if you could spend the whole six weeks here!'

'I detect a slight contradiction in those remarks; but, in any case, they cling to this insane notion that they can manage their affairs very nicely without me. A pity, but there it is.'

'Yes, it is a pity, but we had better drop the subject now. I see the check cap of our own little private criminologist about to cross the road. Something tells me we should do well not to inflame that over-heated imagination more than we must.'

'We may as well talk about pots and kettles instead,' Robin suggested.

We lunched in a small restaurant just off the boulevard, the gilt on our delicious gingerbread being only faintly tarnished by the predominance of English voices; and then gawped our way round the Orangerie, in the company of three hundred other tourists. After that we strolled up the Champs Elysées for reviving Kyrs at Fouquet's; but the only film which found favour in all eyes was playing at a cinema in Montparnasse. So we crossed the river again and finished the day with dinner at the Coupole. The scintillating feature here was the heavy sprinkling of French people among the customers, making us feel that, after all the slog, we belonged to Paris at last.

The flat was like a new pin when we returned, more than ten hours after leaving it, and Robin's shirt from the previous day had been laundered and placed on his bed.

'Good old Lupe!' I said, with a jaw-splitting yawn. 'Do you think we could persuade her to come and live in Beacon Square?'

'I trust not,' Robin replied. 'If it's true that she has either four or eight children.'

'I wouldn't say this to anyone but you, but I don't rely too heavily on Ellen as interpreter. It could well be that Lupe only wishes she had four children and her sister wishes she had eight; or vice versa.'

'Nevertheless,' he replied, 'they sound to me the kind of wishes that are all too likely to be fulfilled, and that is not a thing I would choose to occur at Beacon Square. You look exhausted. Goodnight and sleep tight.'

'Oh, I will. As a drum. And I hope to dream of practical ways of rounding up all those spies. Since we seem to be stuck with Mr Carlsen, we may as well use him to get a foot in the door. If I bring it off, I should think it would get you the Légion d'Honneur, at least, if not the Freedom of Paris and the Croix de Guerre . . . and . . .'

I suspect that I had become the target of some stern looks at this point, plus dire warnings on the subject of what he chooses to call meddling; but I cannot prove it, having fallen asleep even before the sentence was completed.

THREE

(i)

SUNDAY was another halcyon day and we went racing at Longchamps. The outing provided two unexpected features and the first was Ellen's flair for picking winners. Her success in this sphere was so breathtaking that after the third race Robin and I gave up all pretence of competing. On the way back from the stands we placed our stakes in her eager little hand, with instructions to place them on the heads of any animals she took a liking to.

This enabled us to return to our table inside and watch the proceedings on the closed-circuit television, an amenity which had been thoughtfully provided for punters like ourselves who were too timid or self-indulgent to face the hurly-burly outside. The camera concentrated mainly on full-screen close-ups of the Tote Board, flicking now and again to lists of the runners and starting price, but such fill-in shots as there were could have been specifically designed to soothe the fears of nervous chaperones. The colour was insipid as a child's painting book; there were no scenes of frenzied crowds; hardly any, come to that, of horses, except as fuzzy blobs galloping away towards a rustic windmill near the starting post.

The favourite background shot was of a massed bank of hydrangeas, which I had noticed just inside the main entrance, about a quarter of a mile from where we were sitting. At one point, just after Ellen had left us again to collect our winnings from the fourth race, we saw a man and a woman posed against this scene, in intimate conversation. It was easy to see why the cameraman lingered so lovingly on them. She was an elegant, dark-haired creature, very chic in a scarlet coat, and he wore a pale green suit and had a youthful, well-scrubbed face under a shock of snow-white hair. Set against the celestial back drop of flowers and sky, they made an arresting picture, and I was about to say to Robin, when he said furiously:

'For God's sake, Tessa, just look at that! Is there no escape?'

'From what?' I asked, looking around me.

'Those Carlsens. No, that's right, you didn't meet her, but that's Mrs Carlsen in the red coat.'

I practically fell across the table in my eagerness, but already there had been a camera switch and we were back with the picturesque old windmill. The sight of it no longer brought any comfort.

'Damn it all, Robin, what does she mean by slipping off to private assignations and leaving that Sven to rampage around on his own? And where's Ellen got to? She should have been back by now.'

'Keep calm,' he said, his own burst of irritation evaporating as mine began to boil up, 'I expect it's just an unlucky coincidence because thousands of people go to Longchamps, so why not them? Probably they've only just arrived and it's his turn to park the car today.'

'People don't arrive in time for just the last two races. It's a plot, I'm sure of it. Perhaps he followed us here and now he's given his wife the slip. Honestly, I do think one of us ought to go and look for Ellen.'

'I will, if you're really worried. Just so long as you don't want me to find a post office while I'm out there and send a cable to Toby. Oh look! All's well. Here she is.'

'What a relief!' I said. 'But I'm taking no more chances if you don't mind. I think we should go home now.'

Ellen had not done quite so well on the fifth race and I made this the excuse to break things up:

'Always bring the curtain down before they've had enough of you,' I said pompously. 'It's one of the cardinal rules.'

'Did you come across anyone you knew in that mob?' Robin asked her casually, when we were driving home.

'No, but how could I? Lupe's the only person I know in Paris and I expect she's too busy with the children to go to race meetings.'

'You know Mr Carlsen,' I reminded her.

'Oh yes, but I don't count him. He's really more your friend than mine. What are we doing this evening?'

'Oh blimey! Haven't we had enough excitement for one day?'

'No, not nearly.'

'How about a thrilling game of international scrabble?' Robin suggested. 'You could play in Spanish, Tessa in French and I'll stick to English. That might be both edifying and exciting.'

'As well as giving you the best chance of all for a bit of cheating,' I pointed out, but even this bait proved resistible.

'Can't we go somewhere and have some singing and dancing? I want to fritter my winnings.'

She was a true child of her father and, like him, invariably got her own way, although the singing and dancing which was even then lying in wait for us, however much an improvement on the trilingual scrabble programme, may not have been quite the variety she had in mind.

When we arrived back at the flat we found the corner of an envelope protruding from under the front door. It was addressed to Robin and me and contained a smudgy, roneoed sheet of paper, announcing that someone called Vishnaradhakrishna would be appearing for one performance only with his celebrated company, at seven forty-five on Sunday, at 19 rue de la Cavallerie, in a recital of Indian music and dance. Admission 15 Fr.

Pinned to it was a handwritten note, also in English, which ran as follows:

Dear Friends,

Sven Carlsen (a colleague of my husband's) feels you will be interested in the enclosed. Unfortunately, neither he nor Adela can be with us tonight, but we do hope you will both come. Vishna is a beautiful person and one of the finest musicians of our day. Your presence would mean so much and I look forward to welcoming you to our little gathering.

Sincerely, Leila Baker

'Oh, another little machination on the part of the one Ellen calls our friend,' Robin said in a disgusted tone. 'I wonder how much more of it I can stand?'

'It might be a smart move to go, however, since it's the one place in Paris tonight where we can be sure of not finding him.'

'Oh, I know you always fall for phrases like: "Your presence would mean so much," but fifteen francs! You'd have thought, if it meant as much as that, she could have sent us complimentary tickets.'

'Perhaps it wouldn't mean quite so much, if we weren't paying,' Ellen pointed out. 'At any rate, it would be better than just sitting at home all the evening. What do you say, Tessa? My treat!'

'I have a strong feeling it won't be mine,' Robin told her. 'And where is this Cavalry Road, anyway? Miles away, probably.'

'Just round the corner, actually.'

'Oh well, in that case, at least there'll be time for a shower first and a nice big drink. Something tells me I'm going to need every drop of them.'

(ii)

There might have been time for one but strictly speaking there wasn't time for two nice big drinks, and we crept furtively into 19 rue de la Cavallerie ten minutes after the scheduled time.

It had turned out to be an annexe of IDEAS, one of three or four separate buildings within its grounds and accessible from them, but with another entrance on to the side street. I concluded that this enabled it to function as a conference hall for official use and also to earn its keep by being hired out at weekends for occasions such as this, which carried the blessing, if not the banner of the organisation. At any rate, there was no mention of IDEAS in any of the newspaper reports which dealt with the major event of the evening.

However, at five minutes to eight this was still in the future and nothing could have looked less ominous than the scene in the foyer, when Ellen and I sidled in, leaving Robin to pay the taxi. It had been agreed that, for appearances' sake, he would shell out all the expenses of the evening and present his account later.

The entrance hall was a lofty, austere kind of place, with a marble floor and mahogany panelling. There were two or three dozen people dotted around in groups, looking somewhat lost and subdued by the grandeur of their surroundings. They included a few Europeans and one or two Africans as well, but the majority were Indian, all in national dress. There were even a few veiled women of unidentified nationality, looking more like novice nuns than people in search of entertainment, who added an extra solemnity to the atmosphere. I assumed that their presence signified that the occasion had some religious or mystical contribution for the initiates, although I could have been as much mistaken in this conclusion as in another which I had jumped to even earlier. I had taken all these people to be latecomers like ourselves, waiting for the first item on the programme to finish, before disturbing the audience inside, but in fact the double doors to the auditorium stood wide open, revealing a silent and darkened interior.

Robin entered Centre, looking harassed and distraught. He had grown increasingly harassed and distraught ever since the outing was mooted, so I did not take much account of it; but instead of joining us he grabbed my arm and drew me back towards the entrance:

'Are you sure the Carlsens won't be here?' he demanded in shaky tones.

'No, of course I'm not. I only know what the letter said, and you read it, too. Why? Have you seen them?'

'Not exactly. It's just that there's a whole covey of C.D. cars parked outside and for a moment I wondered . . .'

'Well, there's been no sign of them so far, and anyway practically everyone here is foreign, so I expect they mostly come from embassies and so on.'

'Yes, you're quite right. One must try not to get obsessive about it. Come on, then. Let's get it over, shall we? Where's the box office?'

'There isn't one. Nothing commercial like that. I think you're supposed to get the tickets from that female dragon over there. Do you think it's Mrs Baker, in person?'

The middle-aged, severe-looking woman I referred to was seated behind a table in the middle of the room, with rolls of tickets and typewritten sheets spread out before her, and she had had us under observation for some minutes. Commercial or not, she had certainly mastered the universal box office trick of keeping the customer in his place: 'Have you reserved the places?' she snapped, as Robin approached.

She spoke in a clear, precise English, but with a marked French accent and I rejected all idea that she might be Mrs Baker. Whoever had penned our letter of invitation had been of Anglo-Saxon origin, and also rather soppy; two things which this ticket dispenser most definitely was not.

'I don't think so. At least, it's possible, I suppose. That is, if seats have been reserved for us, it would have been done by Mrs Baker. I expect you know her?'

'But of course. What is your name, please?'

'Oh yes, how silly . . . Price. The name is Price,' he repeated in the firmer tone of one who is proud to be positive about something.

She consulted one of her typed lists, while Robin continued to explain himself:

'There might be only two seats in that name,' he said, allowing a note of hope to creep in, 'We are three, as it happens, but it wouldn't matter a bit because . . .'

It was a doomed hope, however, for she cut him short: 'No, there is nothing here, but we have some places available. If you are three, this will be forty-five francs.'

He handed it over and turned back to Ellen and me: 'Well, what now? I don't suppose there's a bar, is there?'

'Not a chance. Let's go inside and take the weight off our feet.'

I did not add: 'And get it over,' partly to spare Ellen's feelings and partly because I did not possess his insane optimism. Since there was no evidence at all that the proceedings were even about to begin, it would have been premature to concern oneself with when they would finish.

Our seats were about six rows back, on the centre aisle, but the allocation must have been fairly elastic, because a white-robed, heavily veiled woman, who had been the sole occupant of that row, got up and removed herself to the one behind, when we sat down. As a matter of fact, every member of the audience could have had a row of seats to himself, had he felt so inclined, for it was a vast, circular hall capable of holding up to a thousand people, and there were only about the same number inside as had been standing in the foyer.

No one offered us a programme and our only clue to the treats in store was provided by the props on the uncurtained stage. This was really just a low platform, lighted from above by a single chandelier, and with an oriental rug spread out over the centre of it. Some cushions had been placed on this rug, together with various instruments, one of which, Ellen kindly informed Robin, was a sitar; a fact which he kindly pretended not to have known.

Downstage, on the O.P. side, there was a lectern with a shelf above it, holding a carafe and tumbler and a pair of spectacles.

There were also numerous people of both sexes and in a variety of costumes wandering about on stage, including one brilliantly-dressed, bare-footed girl, with an expression of deep abstraction on her face, who was practising dance steps. Most of the others were fussing about with the props, constantly arranging and rearranging them, only to have the arrangement upset a minute later by someone else; but all oblivious, it seemed, of each other and of the shadowy figures dotted around in the audience.

Nevertheless, our arrival did not pass entirely unobserved. We had only been sitting there for a few minutes when a dumpy woman detached herself, left the platform by one of the pair of steps which flanked it on either side and came speeding up the aisle towards us. I had taken her for an Indian, for she wore a plain cotton sari and her hair was pulled back into two long, thick plaits hanging down her hack, but at close view her features and colouring were unmistakably European. Moreover, when she spoke it was with a curious mid-Pacific intonation and an accent which hovered between Australian and American.

'I'm Leila,' she announced, seizing both my hands and holding on tightly. 'And you must be Theresa! How good you could come!'

'Awfully kind of you to invite us,' I mumbled, rather fazed by her joyous intensity. 'This is my husband, Robin, by the way, and my cousin Ellen.'

'Hi, there, Robin and Ellen!' she cried, favouring each of them with an ecstatic smile, but not releasing my hands, even when Robin nobly proffered one of his own as bait.

'I know you'll find this will be a great, great experience for you,' she went on, leaning right over him so that her face practically touched mine, as she gazed earnestly into my eyes. 'Something tells me you are a truly receptive person and Vishnaji has this transcendental quality of getting straight to people's hearts and souls. It cuts right through all the little lies and pretences which we ordinary folk try to build up around ourselves.'

I was completely stumped for a suitable reply to this, but Robin, who had not neglected to build up a few lies and pretences along the way, murmured that we were all looking forward to it; could hardly wait, in fact.

A handful more people came sauntering in from the foyer at this point, which was a break for me because as they passed by Mrs Baker let go of my hands, in order to place her own together, palms facing, as she tipped her head forward in the Indian salute.

'Vishnaji has been meditating for some time,' she went on, returning to the attack, 'but something tells me he will soon be ready for us. I shall go and see. Goodbye, dear people. Let us meet again soon.'

Whereupon, she repeated the hand movement, tilted her head to each of us in turn and trotted off, back to the platform. Her solid form had obscured our view of it during the past few minutes, but with her departure we found that things had taken a giant step forward. All the stage hands had vanished and the players had come on. There were two of them, an elderly, aesthetic-looking man, and a round-faced, jolly-looking plump one, both wearing white dhotis.

Having disposed themselves cross-legged on the cushions, the older man drew the sitar across his knees, while the other rested his incongruously slim and sinewy wrist on the tabla, closed his eyes and fell into an attitude of rapt stillness. Mrs Baker took her place behind the lectern.

'Good evening, dear friends,' she began, after bowing first to the musicians and then to the audience, and proceeded to introduce the first number, which was to be a raga. This as her somewhat laboured explanation revealed, was in the nature of variations on a traditional melody, which evolved spontaneously and could therefore only be executed by people who had spent many years making music together and were so closely attuned as to achieve perfect harmony of mood. Since it then transpired that there were approximately sixty-seven different moods to choose from, one could not doubt that she was right.

I also gained the impression, and so, judging by the waves of gloom which emanated from him, did Robin, that since this kind of spontaneous composition had no formal beginning it might well go informally on for ever and ever. However, we were not destined to find out, for Mrs Baker conducted her discourse with more enthusiasm than expertise and it became increasingly difficult to concentrate on her words. She regularly repeated herself, dropping her voice at the end of sentences and straying from the point.

Finally, she lost the thread and her voice at one stroke and, after much choking and hand flapping, possibly to indicate that she was not through with us yet, she managed to tilt the carafe over the tumbler. Unfortunately, despite all the preliminary caperings, this was one little item which every single member of the company had overlooked and the carafe was empty.

Responding to her frenzied beckonings, a young man eventually wandered on from the wings and removed the carafe and, after another distressing pause, brought it back again. Mrs Baker took a hearty swig, mopped her face and her spectacles and was at last able to resume.

During all this time the two musicians had remained immobile as statues, although the elder one swayed gently back and forth, as though a stiff breeze had loosened his hold on the plinth. No doubt, they had both long ago mastered the art of transporting themselves to the astral plane during ordeals of this nature, but others of us were not so fortunate. The best I could find in the way of diversion was to observe the reactions of such members of the scattered audience who were near enough to come under scrutiny.

One who no longer belonged in this category was the solitary veiled woman, for we had not been the only ones to scare her off. A second or two after Mrs Baker left us I had heard someone move into the seat behind Robin's and from the corner of my eye had noticed the mysterious hooded figure get up and shuffle away. I had concluded when we first saw her that she had been temporarily abandoned by some husband or brother finding himself obliged to depart on an errand where she could not follow him, but now, with only a fraction of my attention held by Mrs Baker's interminable monologue, it struck me as an odd thing that one whose normal habitat was so patently the harem should be out on the loose in a public place and darting around as the whim dictated.

On the other hand, this kind of logical thought-process was rapidly becoming out of place, for the whole proceedings had begun to take on an inconsequential, dreamlike quality, where the laws of cause and effect had ceased to operate and whose impressions would fade away on the instant of waking. The next minute it became shot through with a nightmare quality, as well.

I had shifted slightly in my seat, so as to catch an unobtrusive glance at the newcomer behind us, and found myself staring straight into the pale blue eyes of the young-faced, white-haired man, last seen beside the hydrangea bed at Longchamps.

There was really nothing to be so alarmed at in this, but the shock came from the fact that, instead of returning my look with indifference or mild curiosity, which would have been normal in the circumstances, he looked straight back at me, as insolently and knowingly as if it were I who had been featured on the television screen and he inside, watching me.

I instantly turned my head away, and only then became aware that Ellen and Robin had leant forward and were gawping at the stage, and also that Mrs Baker was no longer addressing us.

She had her back to the audience, one hand gripping the lectern, the other shielding her eyes from the light of the chandelier. Moreover, the tabla player had broken out of his trance-like state and was bending over his elderly partner; and it was the behaviour of this one which had evidently

produced a crisis on stage and caused rippling murmurs of
alarm to spread through the house.

The old man's arms were now wrapped around his stomach and his shoulders hunched, as he jerked back and forth
on his haunches. There was nothing rhythmic or serene in
these movements; they were all too obviously the agonised,
involuntary writhings of someone in severe physical pain.

Mrs Baker moved a step or two upstage and simultaneously the fat man laid a hand gently on the other's
shoulder, causing him to keel over sideways and crumple
on to the carpet.

Letting out a wild scream, Mrs Baker staggered forward
and might have collapsed on top of him, had not the fat
man caught her in time and held her off. Twisting in his
grasp, she turned to face the audience and, choking on the
words, yelled out:

'A doctor . . . doctor! Oh, please, someone! Can't you see
Vishnaji is ill? Is there a doctor?'

Surprisingly enough, in view of the size of the audience,
there appeared to be at least twenty, including two women,
and even before her words were out they were leaping up
from all parts of the hall and hurtling on to the stage. Among
the first to reach it was my white-haired friend from the row
behind, and it was he who dragged Mrs Baker away, before
returning to join the fray.

Robin had also leapt up, though for a different reason:
'Come on, both of you,' he said. 'We'd better go.'

I started to obey, but Ellen seemed reluctant to move.

'Is he dead?' she asked in an interested voice.

'Shouldn't think so for a moment, but there are more
than enough people coping with it and nothing we can do.
Come on, there's a good girl.'

She rose and followed us into the aisle, but not quite fast enough. After a brief consultation with all the others crowding round the patient, a young man came down to the edge of the platform. He held up his hand for the silence he already had, and we were obliged to sit down again. He was obviously getting a small thrill from the drama of the situation and of his own moment in the limelight, so it would have been unfair to walk out on him, but fortunately he knew enough to keep it short.

He informed us that Vishnaradhakrishna was suffering from a mild heart attack, but there was no cause for alarm and the ambulance had been summoned. He then apologised to us all for our disappointment and begged us to retreat in good order.

I cannot claim that Robin's or my disappointment was of the kind to leave permanent scars, but I am sure neither of us would have chosen to be released in such a way and the moan of sirens as we came out into the street struck a further chill to the heart.

'Never mind,' he said, with unnatural heartiness, 'he'll soon be on his way now, and, like the man said, it's probably nothing serious.'

'You surely didn't believe all that stuff, did you?' Ellen asked scornfully. 'I saw everything that happened and I bet you what you like that poor old Vishna is dead already.'

She was probably right, too, although the brief description of the dolorous event which appeared in the morning papers stated that he had suffered a coronary attack and had died before reaching the hospital.

As it happened, he must have been an eminent personage in more eyes than Mrs Baker's, because one reporter added that his body was to be flown to India that very day, where many thousands of mourners waited with heavy hearts to receive it.

FOUR

(i)

'REALLY most unpleasant,' Sven agreed, as we surveyed the bedraggled glories of the Italian garden through sheets of rain which cascaded down the plate-glass windows of IDEAS, 'and I'm most fearfully sorry that you were involved in it. I'm afraid I was largely to blame for that. Poor Leila does rather pester one to rally round for all these good Works of hers and when I chanced to mention that I'd met you there was no holding her. She simply wouldn't give up until she'd wormed your address out of me. I do hope I'm forgiven for letting her have it? I knew it wouldn't commit you to anything and Leila's importunities don't usually land one in disasters on that scale.'

'She was the one we felt most sorry for, as it happens. It can't be much fun to have your leading man drop dead at your feet, so to speak. I think she was pretty knocked out.'

'Yes, I am sure. She takes life very hard, poor Leila, and she is not a very happy person at the best of times. Even quite small mishaps get her down and I am afraid she will be in a frantic state today. She has certainly not come to work, which is perhaps a good thing.'

'Oh, does she work here? We understood it was her husband.'

'They both do. Leila's in our personnel department, which gives her plenty of scope for getting in most people's hair for much of the time. No, no, I am fond of her really, and I mustn't be spiteful. Whatever will you think of me?'

I could hardly tell him that, so asked instead what kind of work Mr Baker did at IDEAS.

'Reg? Oh, he's in my division now. He comes from Adelaide, I believe, but he's been all over the place. London was their last posting and I gather that's where Leila picked up some of her rather bogus oriental notions.'

'But now they're here permanently?'

'Ah, that I couldn't say. He's only on a six-month contract, so far, and I'm not sure that rolling stone is ready yet to gather some moss. I'm not even sure how much he enjoys being a small fish in this rather big pond. I say, you are a wizard at drawing out indiscretions, aren't you? I shall have to watch my step. Let's turn to safer subjects. What a charming cap your cousin's wearing. It makes her look so deliciously gamine. I am sure my stepson will be entranced.'

'Your stepson?'

'Yes, he's been persuaded to join our little party, for once. I don't need to tell you who is responsible for that. When he heard Theresa Crichton would be there . . .'

'I had no idea it was to be a party,' I said ungraciously, irritated by his assumption that I both needed constant flattery and was taken in by it. 'Who else is coming?'

'Well, Adela, of course, who is dying to meet you.'

'How old is her son, by the way?'

'Jonathan? Nearly eighteen. He's been spending part of his vacation with us.'

'He doesn't go to school in France?'

'No, he only comes to us for a few weeks in the summer. His father is in America.'

'You and your wife haven't any children of your own?'

'Alas, no. Do you feel strong enough to come and take a look at our Matisse?'

'By all means. Does it need strength? Is anyone else coming to lunch?'

He had darted a pace or two ahead of me as I spoke and it seemed that the question had not been heard; but then he stopped and turned round.

'Just two others, as it happens. I find my wife has invited some friends of hers, people called Müller. He works in my department, too, and Thea's English. I expect Adela thought you'd be glad of one compatriot among all us polyglots.'

He glanced at me enquiringly, as though waiting for me to confirm or deny it. Feeling disinclined to do either, I said nothing, and he went on in a sudden, awkward rush: 'Franz was a celebrated T.B. specialist, with his own clinic, but nowadays all his work is done here.'

'You surprise me,' I admitted.

'Why so?' he asked sharply.

'I thought it was one of the diseases which had been more or less wiped out.'

'Ah, my dear, I am afraid that is only true of our over-privileged Western countries. In some parts of the world it is still very much a factor. IDEAS help to support several hospitals and mobile units and we also have quite an ambitious educational programme. There's the Matisse,' he went on, pointing to a wall ahead of us. 'Some people say it looks like the bathroom wallpaper, but do say you agree with me that it's really rather delightful.'

'I'm a bit stumped,' I confessed. 'I'm sure I'd like it better if you hadn't given me such a precise reason why I shouldn't.'

'Somehow, I feel sure your husband will have a more positive opinion.'

'I'm sure of it, too. Do go and ask him.'

*

'The damnedest part of it is,' I said, drawing Ellen aside, 'that his wife and stepson will be lunching with us, too; not to mention a few more polyglots.'

'Which is the damnedest part of all that?'

'The whole lot, because it more or less obliges us to invite the Carlsens back. If he'd been on his own we could have slid out of it, on the grounds that Robin was leaving tomorrow. Now he's dragged the family in and made a formal sort of party, we'll be even more involved.'

'There is something I feel bound to tell you,' Sven said, panting up to my side again, having evidently prised a satisfactory positive verdict out of Robin. 'The fact is, your question about Franz put me in rather a quandary.'

'I'm sorry. That was the last thing I intended.'

'Not your fault at all, but I've been thinking it over and I feel I should warn you not to ask him anything about his past career.'

'Why? Is he an old lag or something?'

'Well, the idiotic thing is that he is, in a way, but please don't get the wrong idea. He was something of a hero to many people, but politically he was considered undesirable. Rather too liberal, you know. Finally, he was arrested and sent to prison for manslaughter. A completely trumped-up charge, I need hardly say. One of his patients was supposed to have died through negligence, or some such nonsense. Anyway, he naturally had no wish to remain in Germany after his release, and no means of building up a new practice abroad, which is how he comes to be here. I thought I should mention it.'

I wished he hadn't, though. I felt sorry for the poor old doctor, but presumably the subject of crime and punishment had cropped up from time to time in his hearing, and he had learnt to live with it. The chances of my introducing it inadvertently had been about a million to one, until categorically instructed not to, when they had instantly shortened to odds on. The only effective solution for a dilemma of this kind was to tear this page from my mind and replace it with a blank one, which is not so difficult to do, once you have mastered the trick, an invaluable one, in fact, for an actor taking on a classical role which he has seen performed innumerable times by other people. In this case, the process got a helping hand from the fact that the clean new page very soon had some writing on it. It had occurred to me that the story of Dr Müller's imprisonment was most likely pure fabrication and exactly the kind of tale that someone would invent, if he had come to Paris to do a bit of spying.

(ii)

Adela Carlsen and her son were waiting for us at a table in the bar. He had the same dark hair as his mother, although hers was short and curly and his worn in a more dégagé style, tumbling over his face and shoulders. So far as one could see behind this heavy curtain, his face was set in a mould of chronic discontent. There was no question that Adela had been the woman at Longchamps and she even wore the same scarlet coat, to clinch it.

She greeted Robin like an old friend, only later turning to me to ask if I knew someone in London called Milly Carpenter. I denied it and visibly descended several notches in her social scale.

'It's a big place,' I said defensively, 'with a lot of people.'

'Oh, but Milly gets around simply everywhere. Why, she must know more people in the theatre . . . She's a darling person, you'd love her. I'm always trying to get her to come over and visit in Paris for a while, but she's too damn taken up with the social whirl, I guess.'

'Can't you go and see her in London?'

'Used to. We had some really marvellous times together. But now we have the two babies, and Sven not home all day . . .'

My reproachful look at Sven elicited the information that the babies were a pair of poodles, around whom their lives revolved. I noticed that in his wife's presence he adopted a slight American intonation, which had not been in evidence before; a tribute, maybe, to her forceful personality, perhaps just another manifestation of being all things to all men.

'Not while they have those damn quarantine laws,' Adela informed me.

I think I may have started to turn purple in the face at this point, because Robin chipped in with some dreary anecdote about a poodle belonging to his mother, which he had certainly never thought worth mentioning before.

Jonathan, meanwhile, had not uttered a word, although I had noticed some surreptitious glances at Ellen from beneath the thunderous black eyebrows; and Sven had been making noisy but ineffectual attempts to get our orders for the bar. He was in the final stages of sorting this out when we were joined by the other two guests.

Mrs Müller was even more beautiful than Adela, as well as a year or two younger. She had auburn hair and blue eyes and wore a plain, black linen dress, the simple effect being saved from downright dullness by one or two well-placed diamonds. She shook her head to Sven's offer of a drink and Adela was on her feet in an instant, saying that since we were now all assembled and she had been obliged to leave the dogs shut up in the car, it would be advisable to cut out the apéritifs and go straight in to lunch. She then dashed through the introductions, linked arms with Thea Müller and led the way to the restaurant.

This was in the style of a huge conservatory, jutting out from one end of the long narrow building, like the sun deck over the stern of a ship, and it took us three or four minutes to walk there from the bar. Once more, I found myself paired off with Sven in this procession, and suspecting that Adela might have another, undisclosed reason for being in such a tearing hurry, I had a whim to ask him if he happened to know the white-haired man with the boyish face, who had entered the bar just before we left.

'Oh, what a delightful description!' he exclaimed, reverting instantly to his archaic public-school English. 'It could only fit one person. Yes, of course I know him, although, as I told you, he's only been here quite a short time.'

'Did you tell me that?' I asked stupidly.

'Yes, I'm positive I did, you know. That's Reg Baker. Leila's husband.'

'So I hear you had some not so nice experience for your first days in Paris?' Dr Müller said, as we sat down to lunch.

He was a large, grizzly-bear sort of man, with a bluff jolly manner and twinkly blue eyes; not quite the conventional spy figure of the seedy mac and homburg, but you can't always rely on type-casting.

'You mean the poor old man and his heart attack? Yes, it was a horrid thing to happen, but I can't pretend we were personally involved. You weren't at the concert, were you?'

'No, I am glad to say. Leila tried very hard to make us go, but it was not possible. She is very persistent, you know, so it was not easy to back out, but I think in the end Thea took some tickets, just to pacify her. Isn't that so, my dear?'

Mrs Müller, who was sitting opposite me on Sven's left, nodded briefly, but did not put herself to the wear and tear of replying aloud.

'Well, you didn't miss anything,' I said, speaking to neither of them in particular.

'No, and this is one time when virtue is rewarded. I think we must have gone, if I had not been obliged to stay at home and do some work.'

'Really? On Sunday night?'

'Oh yes, this can happen, you know. There is a big meeting this afternoon, which has to be prepared for, and sometimes the only way to get down to such things without interruption is at home. But why do we talk of work at such a time? You have been making some pleasant excursions in Paris, as well, hein?'

'Yes, lots. We had a fabulous day at the races.'

'Ah, that is good. So you won some money?'

'I didn't, but my cousin was very lucky; or so it seemed at the time. How about you, Sven?' I asked, hoping the question sounded natural. 'Did you have any winners yesterday?'

'Winners?' he repeated blankly.

'Robin thought he saw you at Longchamps yesterday.'

'Did he? Then I must have been sleepwalking. I am ashamed to confess that I spent the whole of yesterday afternoon recuperating from the night before.'

'Then it must have been your wife he saw. I expect I got it wrong.'

He shook his head: 'No, I assure you. Adela was exercising the dogs, as she does every afternoon. In fact, if memory serves, she drove out to Saint-Cloud and walked them in the park there. It's very beautiful at this time of year. You must let us take you and your cousin out one Sunday. You would enjoy it.'

'Not if she is a true Englishwoman,' Dr Müller said, wagging his head knowingly. 'They do not care for our continental parks where everything is orderly and symmetrical. Thea is always complaining about this. She misses the wildness you find in your English gardens, is it not so?'

I looked again at Thea, who had acknowledged these remarks about her with a faint smile. She did not strike me as one who went in for wildness very seriously, and I wondered whether her impassively silent manner arose naturally from her temperament, or had been cultivated as a youth and looks preserver. There were signs that the latter might be her abiding passion in life, for she had waved away the bread and potatoes and was now neatly dissecting her sole meunière and pushing most of it to one side of her plate. Also she was drinking mineral water instead of wine.

This also applied to Adela, but even with two total abstainers the three bottles of wine which Sven had ordered did not quite last out, and in fact he drank almost a whole one on his own. He was gesturing to the waiter for fresh supplies when Adela intercepted him. She said that she didn't have too much time and had promised faithfully to take the babies for walkies in the Champ de Mars. A few minutes later she was on her feet and, with impassioned reminders to Robin about our all getting together again next time he was in Paris, brought the party to an end.

It was still pouring with rain when we descended to the main hall and Dr Müller insisted on driving us home. We protested that we only had a few hundred yards to go and could easily take a taxi, or even walk, but he would not hear of it. Laughing delightedly, he told us that the district was notorious for its dearth of taxis and that, since he had every intention of driving his wife home, it would not be putting him to the slightest trouble.

It was rather mystifying after all this to find ourselves being ushered back into the lift, where he pressed a bell marked S.2., but he explained that his was the lower of the two basement floors and was used as a car park.

'So nobody is getting their feet wet,' he said, as we emerged into the Stygian caves. 'And since you are all not so fat like me, there will be plenty of room.'

No one could deny this, for his car turned out to be a sleek and powerful Mercedes, with what Robin had described as those distinctive green number-plates.

Ellen sat in front and Frau Müller placed herself beside Robin and me, leaning well back in her corner, as though we were a couple of particularly unappetising soles meunières.

It was interesting to find that the doctor, who had projected the jolly, rumbustious image all through lunch, became a demon of aggression when seated behind the wheel. He ricocheted in and out of traffic lanes, blaring his horn at startled pedestrians and shooting across amber lights like a man possessed. None of this appeared to ruffle Thea in the least: 'Give them an inch and they'll take an ell,' she remarked impassively, as Simcas and Renaults fell back in disorder all around us.

'Have you known the Carlsens long?' I asked her, more to divert my own mind from these cavortings on the slippery roads than from genuine curiosity.

'Oh, Franz knew him ages ago. Neither of us had seen Adela until we came to Paris. When did you first meet Sven, Franz?'

'In the dark ages, my darling. Do you wish these young people to know how ancient I am? His first wife was my patient. So! This is your house, ja?'

'Yes, and thanks for the lift.'

'We meet again, I hope. Auf wiedersehen.'

*

'Who has the keys?' Robin asked, fumbling through his pockets, as we stood outside the front door.

'You have,' we both replied.

'How very disappointing! I thought so, too, but we all seem to be wrong.'

'You transferred them to your macintosh just before we went out,' Ellen told him, 'I saw you.'

'And what became of your macintosh during lunch, Robin?'

'Oh God, you don't think your friend has been up to his tricks again? He took it off me and put it in his office.'

'Didn't you go with him?'

'No, why should I? It seemed a perfectly normal thing to do.'

Luckily, Lupe was still in the flat and was prevailed upon by Ellen to let us in. Robin marched straight to the telephone and was eventually connected with a Mademoiselle Pêche, which struck me as a charming name for a secretary, although he said that this one sounded more like a quince than a peach. She informed him that Mr Carlsen had gone to a meeting outside the building and would not be available until five o'clock. She promised to pass on Robin's enquiry about the keys, and she must have been as good as her word, for at six o'clock she brought them round, in person.

She turned out to be the censorious, middle-aged lady last seen selling tickets for the Recital of Indian Music and Dance, and once again she was inclined to be severe with us. This time, however, her displeasure was on behalf of Mr Carlsen and the trouble and pain Robin had caused him by allowing the keys to fall out of his pocket. We grovelled a bit, in the face of her disapproval, but did not get so carried away as to refer to the visit of two gallant messieurs from an organisation called S.O.S., who had already performed a rapid and efficient service. By the time that Mademoiselle Pêche handed over the old set of keys, their only remaining function was in unlocking the refrigerator.

FIVE

(i)

ELLEN and I both drove out to Orly to see Robin off on Tuesday. It was an affecting scene, but he told us to dry our eyes and soyez de bon courage, which is no doubt what the gentlemen of the piscine say to each other when they find themselves in deep waters.

Even more cheering was his promise to return for another long weekend before the month was out; so the homeward drive was not so desolate as we had foreseen and, by the end of it, we had so far recovered our spirits as to have laid down plans for our cinema-going the following evening. I was on call at the studios, but only for lighting tests and rehearsals, and expected to be through by six.

Determined to be punctual, if nothing else, on my first working day, I was standing on the pavement, fighting down the nauseating nerves, a good ten minutes before the car was due to collect me. Making an iron pact with myself not to sneak another look at my watch until twenty more people, excluding children, had passed by, I chanced to be in an exceptional situation to perceive the slow and wavering advance of Leila Baker, who, appropriately enough, would have been checked out as number thirteen, if she had only passed by.

Unfortunately she chanced to perceive me, too, and even though she was clearly in a state of mental torment similar to my own, a gleam of recognition lit up her face and she quickened her pace and came alongside.

'Why, Theresa!' she burst out, placing a firm grip on my arm and speaking in such a breathless rush that once again her voice almost deserted her. 'Oh, it is good to see you . . . so wanting to talk with you . . . answer to prayer . . . made up my mind . . . what you must think.'

'Oh no, honestly,' I protested. 'You mustn't worry about us. It was a wretched thing to happen, but you're the one we feel sorry for.'

For some reason, so far from steadying her, this assurance only increased her distress. She still clung tightly to my arm, but it had become a means of support, quite distinct from her natural tactile compulsions, and she swayed a little, swivelling her eyes away from me:

'Do you? For me? No, don't . . . You're such a sensitive, intuitive person, Theresa . . . feel it.'

'Oh no, not really. Are you feeling all right? I'm sorry I can't ask you in, but . . .'

She looked at me, but she was barely listening.

'Is your husband still here?' she asked in a clearer, almost crafty tone, and so much to my astonishment that the major part of mind was momentarily jerked away from the ticking hands of my watch.

'No, he's not. He went back to London yesterday. Why do you ask?'

'It just occurred to me . . . I had a mind to . . . that is, if you . . .'

She was off on the waffle again and my brief flutter of curiosity died away. At the same moment a car on the other side of the street made an intrepid U-turn, missing the nose of a bus by centimetres, and pulled up beside us. Leaning sideways, Pierre flung open the passenger door and embarked on a pantomime of shrugs and grimaces, probably to indicate that he had broken all the traffic laws of Paris by this manoeuvre, and I wrenched my arm from Mrs Baker's grasp.

'Sorry, I must fly, or I'll be late for work. Call me up some evening and we'll have a proper talk. Awfully sorry. Goodbye.'

I did not stop to catch her reactions, but bounded into the car and slammed the door:

'Bonjour, madame. Ça y est?'

'Bonjour, Pierre and roulez, s'il vous plaît,' I replied, and then I looked at my watch.

Altogether, I had spent exactly six minutes on the pavement and we were still four ahead of schedule. Fear gave way to relief, and relief, such is so often the way of things, to a burning resentment. I felt angry with Mrs Baker for barging so ineptly into my life, and angrier still with her for making me feel such a mean pig. It was true that more pressing matters had prevented my lending more than half an ear to all her maunderings, but that was really no excuse. Even a deaf man could have recognised that she was dead scared.

(ii)

It was an exhausting, in parts exhilarating day, packed with the small terrors and triumphs which are normal to such occasions and I did not give more than a passing thought to Leila Baker until nearly ten hours later, when Ellen and I kept our evening rendezvous at the cinema.

The film we had chosen was playing at a newly-opened cinema just off the Etoile, where the décor only, as the saying goes, was worth the price of admission. This was just as well, for about half a million other people had had the same idea and we had to spend ten minutes queueing in the foyer for our tickets.

We managed to while away this period by swapping news and views of the day's events, although I frankly admit that I assumed Ellen to be as little riveted by my experiences as I was by the latest data on the domestic life of Lupe and her sister; but, as usual, I had underestimated her.

The early evening performance had just ended and the circle was emptying fast as we swam graciously upward on the red-carpeted escalator. Its descending twin, some yards to our left, was crammed with passengers, but one figure stood out arrestingly among them. His shabby old overcoat flapped behind him in the familiar fashion and the impression he created of being actually in flight was accounted for by the fact that he was galloping down, two steps at a time.

Since he was patently in a raging hurry and since I had no desire whatever to detain him, it can only have been a reflex action which jerked my hand up and caused my voice to shout his name. He probably heard me, though, for he halted and made a half turn in our direction. A moment later other heads got between us and he must have been swept forward with the crowd making for the exit. I dutifully waited a few minutes after alighting, but to my surprise and relief he did not appear.

'That was Mr Carlsen,' I explained to Ellen, who was hovering at my side, in a fever of impatience to feast her eyes on the ice-cream advertisements, 'I thought he'd seen us.'

'You've got him on the brain. I didn't see him.'

'No, I haven't. My brain is just about the only place where I haven't got him.'

'But, Tessa, you're always thinking you see him, everywhere you go. I heard you saying at lunch the other day that you'd seen him at the races, and he'd been in bed all the time.'

'Well, yes, I admit that, but I invented it, as it happens. This time was real.'

'I bet it wasn't, or he'd have come flying after us. It's like I say, you've got him on your poor old brain.'

'Have it your own way. Luckily it's a matter of supreme unimportance,' I said huffily, and with a sublime confidence which can rarely have been more misplaced.

Six

IT IS not necessary to dwell on the hours spent in the studios during this period, except in so far as they impinged on our private lives. My diligent study of the French language turned out to be superfluous, because I played an English Mees, who had teamed up with a group of students on a hitch-hike to the Dordogne. It was the director's whim that, unlike most people wrestling with a foreign tongue, she was able to reel off great chunks of dialogue, without pause or waver, while retaining a thick, nasal Anglo-Saxon accent. The first I was able to learn by heart: the second, alas, came naturally.

The main departure from routine was that I never had to clock in before eleven in the morning. By the French system, shooting starts at midday and continues almost without a break until eight or nine at night. I am not sure how this custom came about, but it has numerous advantages. For one thing, by the time work begins, everyone is fully awake, so less time is lost through inattention or hangovers, and still less from the endless tea and lunch breaks. It also prevents actors from fulfilling major engagements in the theatre while working on a film, which may be a good thing, and it entirely banishes all the terrors and privations involved in rising at six every morning, in order to be made up and on the set by nine o'clock, which is unquestionably a very good thing indeed.

It was thanks to this routine that I was able to carry over my non-working life by starting each day in a civilised Madame Récamier fashion, with a tray of coffee and rolls, kindly supplied by Ellen, plus a session with the English and French newspapers.

I habitually began with *Figaro*, partly in pursuance of the self-improvement course, which had now got a grip on me, and partly because all the main news was conveniently summarised on the front page. Sometimes I never got beyond the front page, for it promised nothing much inside except details of industrial unrest in Clermont-Ferrand, student unrest at Nanterre and *Figaro* unrest with practically everything; and the temptation to take a peep into the *Daily Mail* was almost irresistible.

However, there were occasional rewards for perseverance and on Thursday morning, two days after Robin's departure, I came across a headline which sent me ripping through the paper in search of the relevant page.

The Champ de Mars was the name which first caught my eye and the fact that a woman had been found dead there naturally heightened the interest, although I managed to keep it down to simmering point by reminding myself that this open space was doubtless used by other members of the public, besides Adela and her poodles. As it happened, a glance confirmed that the dead body which had been bundled under a bench in the shrubbery was not hers. For one thing, the victim, after being knocked unconscious, had been strangled with her own hair. Furthermore, the last

paragraph revealed that she had already been identified as
Madame Leila Baker.

In fact, it was the inconsolable husband who had made
the identification and he had also drawn the attention of
the investigators to the fact that a gold necklace, which his
wife always wore, was missing. This, combined with the
fact that no bag or purse had been found in the vicinity,
manifested that robbery had been the motive. Mrs Baker's
age was given as thirty-seven and she was stated as hailing
from New Zealand.

There followed a stern homily, deploring a state of affairs
which prevented innocent females walking abroad without fear of attack from monstrous assassins, comparable
only to those operating in Chicago under the rule of Al
Capone, but it contained nothing of a factual nature and I
felt too numbed to read it through to the end. Apart from
the natural shock of learning that someone I knew had
been so brutally murdered, there were even more grue-
some emotions to be reckoned with. However hard I tried
to suppress it, the thought would keep returning that when
Mrs Baker had waylaid me in the street, which can only have
been some eight hours before she was killed, it was because
she knew herself to be in mortal danger, and for some totally
incomprehensible reason had sought to confide in me, or
even, impossible as this might seem, to seek my protection.

I tried to rationalise these beliefs out of existence by
reminding myself that she had met her death at the hands
of an unknown assailant after her money and valuables, and
therefore any suspicions she might have held as to what was
in store could only have taken the form of vague premon-
itions of impending doom, whose culmination neither I
nor anyone else could have done anything to avert. It was a
plausible theory, up to a point, for unquestionably much of

her behaviour had been guided by intuition, and it gained colour from Sven's observations concerning her capacity to magnify ordinary mishaps into catastrophic proportions. The shock of Vishna's death, too, would have been a powerful agent in rocking the balance of one who was well known to be emotionally unstable. The only trouble with this comforting theory was that I did not for one instant believe in it, and one of the principle stumbling-blocks was the memory of a curious remark of Ellen's at the concert and which, in the light of this latest development, took on a new and sinister significance.

However, I decided not to probe into this, or even to tell her of Mrs Baker's death, until I had consulted Robin. Owing to the work schedule which I have already described, we had arranged that, except when some predatory female had seized upon my absence to invite him out to dinner, he would telephone me every night at ten o'clock, and that evening his call came through on the dot.

I had discouraged Ellen from listening in on the hand extension, holding communications between man and wife to be more or less sacred, but, not wishing her to feel excluded, had allowed her to remain in the room and make what she could from my end of the conversation.

Quite naturally, she soon grew bored with all the repetitions of 'Oh, are you?', 'Oh, did you?', etcetera, and drifted back to the television. This was the signal for confidential matters to be bruited, and as soon as she had left the room I told him about Leila Baker's death.

Evidently, it had not been reported in the English papers, for he was knocked sideways by the news and, more surprisingly, viewed it with deepest alarm. He went so far as to suggest that I should leave Paris at once.

'But, Robin darling, do be serious. How could I contemplate such a thing? I've signed a contract, you know, and we're scheduled to go on the floor in a day or two.'

'That may not be the only thing on your schedule, by the sound of it. Surely there's still time for them to get someone else for the part?'

'But what reason could I give? You wouldn't honestly expect me to say it was on account of a woman being mugged and murdered in a public park, and I'm not accustomed to that kind of thing? They'd say I was raving mad, and I'd never get another job here as long as I lived. My nom would be boue.'

'Yes, rather appropriate. It strikes me that you've got yourself mixed up with that crowd, whether you like it or not, and there have been far too many unpleasant incidents. I relied on the acquaintance fizzling out when you started work, and now this has to happen! How do we know it was a straightforward mugging job? Those don't usually end with the victim being strangled. They're mostly just knocked unconscious and recover in no time.'

'Well, perhaps that isn't the way it's done in France. The official view is that it was the work of some thug, after her money and her gold necklace, and presumably they base it on a bit more information than they gave out to the Press.'

'And perhaps also the murderer was in full possession of his faculties and realised that the best way to make it look like robbery was to do a bit of robbing. I might add that the so-called official view is not always to be taken at face value. It's quite a convenient stand to take, at this stage, and a way of lulling the real criminal into a false sense of security, as you very well know.'

'Yes, I do know, and I agree with you that it may not be as straightforward as they would have us believe. All the same, I can tell you this much, if it's any comfort to you; whoever killed her, it wasn't Sven Carlsen.'

'Oh? How do you know? You haven't been seeing him again have you?'

'Not in the sense you mean, but one or two fresh items were given out in the evening papers and they put him completely in the clear.'

'Proceed.'

'I've got it in front of me and it says that the local Prefecture were apprised of this miserable occurrence by an anonymous telephone call. Apparently, that's usually the way they do get to hear about these things. Anybody declaring himself to have stumbled on a corpse is liable to be arrested on the spot and clapped into jug for a couple of years, while they sort it out. It can be inconvenient, specially if you happen to be innocent.'

'You exaggerate, of course, but go on. What's all this got to do with Carlsen?'

'Well, Anon, whoever he was, must have been pretty quick off the mark. His call came through at twenty past eight. When the gendarmerie sped to the spot he had indicated, the body was still warm and they estimated that death could not have occurred more than one hour before, which puts the vital time between seven-thirty and eight. Agreed?'

'It doesn't necessarily put it anywhere of the kind, but go on.'

'Why doesn't it?'

'Because death might not have been instantaneous. If your anonymous caller was as scared as you make out, he probably didn't hang around long enough to make sure she was actually dead. Even if he did, it doesn't follow that she died during the attack.'

'Well, honestly, Robin, I don't think it can have been more than minutes afterwards. The Champ de Mars is not exactly the Sahara, you know. Somebody would have noticed her there, specially if there were indications that she was still alive.'

'That's just conjecture, but obviously I'm upsetting some neat little theory of yours which lets Carlsen off the hook, so you'd better tell me what it is.'

'Simply that at ten minutes to eight he was leaving a cinema by the Arc de Triomphe. I don't know how much you remember about the evening traffic in that part of Paris, but I assure you that even Batman couldn't have got from there to the Champ de Mars in under twenty minutes. Even then, he'd have to walk the last part, to the scene of the murder. I haven't checked on how long that would take.'

'And I implore you not to try. I'd much rather you kept out of it. All the same . . .'

'Yes?'

'What if he'd done it in reverse? Supposing the murder had already been committed by the time you saw him? People often claim to have been sitting in a cinema. If they can dig out a ticket and a passable description of the film, it's sometimes rather hard to disprove. I imagine that would not have been beyond Carlsen's ingenuity?'

'No, but it would have been beyond it to get from the Champ de Mars in under twenty minutes, whichever direction he travelled in. There's no direct line to the Etoile by Metro; you have to change at Concorde, which is half an hour's walk, all by itself. If he took the car, he'd have all the bother of parking it twice over, and that would have added another half an hour. The only other way would have been by taxi and you know how hard they are to find in that district. Besides, he would hardly have come running out, brandishing blood-stained weapons, to hail a taxi. The chances are that it would be imprinted on the driver's memory. And, after all that, when he got to the cinema, he would have had to queue for a ticket, as I know for a fact. Anyway, why are you so set against him? I admit he's pursued us rather tiresomely, but that doesn't make him a murderer, does it? And it could all have been true about my suitcase, you know. Come to that, those keys might have dropped out of your pocket by accident.'

'I know, and yet I feel in my bones that there's something tricky about him. Also it is a fact that one of his colleagues has now been murdered and that's not very encouraging, whether he's to blame or not. I'd take it as a favour if you'd keep clear of the whole bunch of them.'

'Of course, I will, Robin; but he isn't involved in this, I promise you.'

'No, you can't. The sort of alibi you've described could contain half a dozen loopholes.'

'But the point is that it wasn't an alibi, in the sense you're implying. He couldn't have had the least idea that Ellen and I would be in the same cinema, and he made no attempt to establish his presence there. On the contrary, it was I who made all the running that time. I'm not even sure that he saw me, but he certainly didn't come back to speak to us.'

I had considered this argument to be so conclusive as to put all Robin's nameless fears to rest, but had reckoned without masculine logic:

'There you are!' he said triumphantly. 'That's just the kind of thing that bothers me. Ever since we met him he's been running after us like a devoted little puppy, and when you suddenly pop up and make it easy for him, what does he do? Ignores you and gallops off in the opposite direction. What are we to make of that?'

'One thing we could make of it, I suppose, is that it was you he was after all the time, and Ellen and I had no part in his schemes.'

I had intended this as a joke, but, strangely enough, he took it seriously.

'Absurd as it may sound, Tessa, the same thought had occurred to me. Though it certainly doesn't add up, unless he's a straightforward crackpot.'

'Not a murdering crackpot, though.'

'Maybe not, but I'd still like you to keep well away.'

'I intend to,' I said, 'and, judging by the last encounter, I don't anticipate the slightest difficulty.'

Ellen came back just after I had replaced the receiver and it flashed through my mind that I had omitted to ask Robin one important question. The telephone rang again almost immediately and I snatched it up, in the firm conviction that his mind-reading abilities were operating just as powerfully at long distance. However, the call was for Ellen.

So then it was my turn to endure all the 'Oh, have you's?' and 'oh, did she's?' and after about the fourth one I left her to it and busied myself in the bathroom for five minutes. When I returned they had reached the: 'Yay, okay . . . kay . . . see you, bye,' stage and I put the inevitable question.

'Only that gloomy Jono,' she replied. 'He's asked me to lunch tomorrow. Is that okay?'

I was rather fascinated to learn that they were on nick-name terms, without, to my knowledge, having exchanged more than two words, but there were more pressing matters than this to be dealt with.

'Seeing I was only two feet away, you could have asked permission first and said the okays later,' I pointed out in governessy tones.

'Oh, sorry, Tess; but you went to lunch with his parents, so I didn't think you'd object. And his mother's in a fantastic stew about this friend of theirs who's been killed, and her husband and everything, so it must be an awful drag for him at home.'

'Yes, it must be, but you're playing it very cool, aren't you? Did you already know about Mrs Baker before Jonathan told you?'

'Yes, it was on the ten o'clock news, when you were talking to Robin. I came in to tell you about it.'

'I see. And is that by any chance why you accepted the invitation with such alacrity? Crichton curiosity getting the better of you?'

She grinned: 'Hark who's talking!'

'Yes, well, there's one other thing I'm curious about, as it happens. When you said Mrs Carlsen was so upset about her friend being killed, why did you add: "And her husband and everything?" Which husband and every which thing?'

'Her own, of course. That's the real bit I came to tell you. Mr Carlsen has been arrested.'

SEVEN

(i)

AT SEVEN the following morning, after a series of nightmares, punctuated by periods of wakefulness, in which the obsession of being fit for nothing the next day became the worst nightmare of all, I struggled to the surface and began to dial our London number.

One hour later, I was still at it, the telephone system having chosen this of all days to be at its most insouciant. Usually the response was total silence, but sometimes I got a shrill, unbroken whine, and sometimes a bell-like jingle played over a voice mechanically repeating some phrase I could not catch. To vary the monotony, I also got a wrong number and found myself holding an unfriendly, not to mention expensive conversation with a gentleman in Maidstone.

After about the tenth try, I gave up that approach and set out to find the operator. This proved successful, up to a point, but unluckily for me she turned out not to be a simple English girl who had married a French aristo, but an articulate, fast-speaking native, who rattled off her instructions with such speed and impatience that I could not follow a word of them.

It was past nine when I finally established contact with Beacon Square, and Robin was no longer there. Our housekeeper informed me that he had not only left, but had taken a suitcase with him, passing the remark that he would be away for several days.

Since he had not passed any such remark to me, I was immediately thrown into a frenzy of alarm and, drowning in this sea of troubles, the question of whether Ellen should or should not be allowed to go out with Jonathan now appeared as a very insignificant ripple on the troubled waters.

'Where's he taking you?' I enquired listlessly, when she appeared with my breakfast tray.

'He's coming here at twelve, but I don't know where we'll go. He says all the places in Paris are a fantastic drag, compared to New York.'

'Well, mind you're back by the time I get in.'

'Listen, Tess, we're only going to have lunch.'

'I know, but one thing can lead to another, even in draggy old Paris, and I feel responsible.'

'So do I,' she replied, regarding me critically, 'and you look shocking. Are you feeling okay?'

'It's just that I slept badly,' I explained. 'Too many things on my mind.'

'I tell you what, then, Tess; if you're really in a stew about it, we needn't go out at all. I'll buzz out and get a few things for lunch and Lupe can cook it for us. She doesn't a bit mind staying late and I promise to turf him out before she goes. How's that?'

'Lovely,' I replied, 'and you're a dear, sweet girl.'

When she had gone I embarked half-heartedly on my morning skirmish with *Figaro*. The news of Sven's arrest was prominently displayed on the front page, but the police were playing it close to the chest. The inside report revealed nothing which I did not already know, while omitting one item which I was becoming increasingly afraid was known to me alone.

Ellen returned, carrying a string bag loaded with provisions, and a stiff grey envelope, which she had found in our mail box. My name and address were inscribed in a large, positive hand, but it was unstamped and we had no means of telling when it had been delivered. Turning first to the signature, I read: 'Adela C.'

There was a Passy address at the top and the message was as follows:

Dear Theresa,

You will have heard the news by the time this reaches you. We are confident the mistake will be cleared up pretty soon, but there is a way you may be able to help in the clarification. I dare not phone, in case our lines are being tapped, but will be home all evening, if you could drop by any time after seven. Sincerely.

I was going through it once again, when Ellen reappeared to caution me about the time.

'Run my bath,' I told her. 'And as soon as I'm dressed I've a letter to write. I want you to give it to Jonathan, with instructions to place it in his mother's hands at the first opportunity.'

I was purposely putting off committing myself until the very last moment, for a hot well-scented bath is often conducive to the bubbling-up of inspiration, and I badly needed one to get me out of this predicament. On the one hand, I had as good as promised Robin not to have any more to do with the Carlsen clan, and personal inclinations also pointed in that direction. On the other, this undertaking had been given before either of us knew that the evidence I alone possessed could save an innocent man from a murder charge. Adela's letter had convinced me that she and Sven were aware of this, too, and that the cause of justice and humanity required my once more embroiling myself in their affairs.

No inspiration came, but further reflection persuaded me that since Robin's partiality for the aforementioned justice and humanity were about as strong as you could find, he could only applaud my decision to speak out.

To prevent further vacillation on the subject, I dashed off a note to say that I would call between eight and nine o'clock that evening. I then repeated my instructions to Ellen and went down to the main entrance, where the car was waiting to drive me to the studios.

(ii)

It was a far more gruelling day than some I have known, and included about fourteen retakes of one short scene, largely because I wasn't concentrating properly, which didn't make it any easier to bear.

We went on later than usual, the rain was beating down as we came out, and the traffic going into Paris was like one enormous, snarling animal. I would have mortgaged my soul to go straight home, put my feet up and have a good cry, and the last straw was piled on by Pierre's total inability to find the Carlsens' house, whose address was 12 bis, rue des Quatre Pigeons. Any fool could have guessed that 12 bis would be situated between numbers 12 and 14, and any fool would have been completely wrong. The house in that position defiantly displayed its blue plaque with the number thirteen for all to see.

Pierre was a dear fellow, but tempestuous by nature, and his approach to every problem was to run about, waving his hands in the air and declaiming to anyone who would listen. After prowling up and down the street for about a quarter of an hour, knocking on doors and getting ticked off by concierges, we eventually located 12 bis at the back of Number 12, approached by what we had taken to be garage doors and forming one side of an elegant courtyard. All very fine when you got there, but who wanted to? Certainly not I, and to be greeted by Dr Müller and two screaming poodles was the last straw bis.

He led me into a low-ceilinged room on the ground floor, with two windows overlooking the courtyard, and furnished in a mixture of French and American styles. There were comfortable, chintzy armchairs, shelves loaded with books and records, and some dashing-looking rugs slung around on the parquet; but the pair of pompous chandeliers and the florid wall brackets had obviously been acquired with the lease.

The central heating was also of the Franco-U.S. variety, consisting of enormous ancient radiators, creaking and gasping like traction engines in their struggle to keep the temperature registered at ninety degrees Fahrenheit.

Adela was suitably attired for this Turkish-bath atmosphere, in a pale blue silk caftan, with strips of gold sandal on her long narrow feet. She looked cross, but no more fearful or unhappy than at our last meeting.

'Why, you finally made it,' she said, stretching forth a languid hand, but not getting up. 'Come right along in and sit down while Franz fixes you a drink. You met Thea already, and this is Reg Baker. Coco, baby, will you please stop that noise and let Mummie speak?'

I planted myself on a sofa beside Mrs Müller, and the second poodle, whose name was Yves, immediately jumped into my lap. Stubbornly resisting my furtive efforts to toss him off, he trod out a nest for himself and curled up for a snooze, which didn't make me feel any cooler.

'Throw him off, if he bothers you,' Adela said, not sounding serious about it.

Dr Müller was standing by a drinks cabinet, making enquiring faces at me, so I asked for a Scotch on all the available rocks. I should have known better, and I did; but there are times in everyone's life when the inner voices nagging on about taking strong drinks on an empty stomach are liable to be ignored, and this was one of them.

Adela, on her own, I could have coped with. Admittedly, her somewhat bored and petulant attitude, so unlike Jonathan's description of the woman in a stew, had rather thrown me; but it takes all sorts, and she had every right to behave as she chose. The difficulty was that, in taking my cue from her, I could only offend the susceptibilities of the bereaved husband. He had gone to the opposite extreme and was obviously under severe emotional stress. He had removed his jacket and, with his straggly damp white hair, white face and white shirt-sleeves, looked as though he had been tricked out for some grotesque soap powder commercial. The boyish look had gone and he was hunched in his chair, tossing back whisky, twitching spasmodically and staring at Adela with pale, bloodshot eyes. Every so often he cleared his throat, as though about to speak, but either thought better of it, or was unable to find the words.

I saw Dr Müller glance at him warily and at one point he went over and placed a reassuring or restraining hand on his arm, murmuring a few words in German, but Adela took no notice of him at all, apparently not even hearing the strangled croaks.

Thea remained as imperturbable as ever, although there was one slight indication that she was not quite so composed as she pretended. One hand mechanically fondled the ears of the second poodle, who stared up at her, glassy-eyed with gratitude.

No one spoke as I lit into my drink and I became gripped by the absurd fear that the combination of hunger and nervous exhaustion would cause my insides to rumble out like a Hammond organ. Getting in first, I said:

'Let me begin by saying how dreadfully sorry I am about all this, but I'm sure you want more than just sympathy and, as you know, I'm here to provide some practical help. I had rather expected your solicitor to be here, but I don't know much about French law, and perhaps the fact that you're all here as witnesses will be enough. If it isn't, I don't mind signing an affidavit, or whatever they call it, and I'm certain that as soon as the police hear what I have to say they will release your husband at once.'

I paused here, not for lack of breath, nor even because the oppressive atmosphere and the discomfort and weight of the dog in my lap were making my heart pound a little, but because I was disconcerted by their reactions. There was no question that I had their full attention. They were moulded into it, like figures in a frieze, but, far from the signs of relief I had looked for, the tension had perceptibly heightened and become more hostile. Even Mrs Müller had stopped stroking the dog, which now whimpered and scrabbled at her legs, and Reg Baker stared at me in open disbelief.

It was frustrating, as well as puzzling, and conscious of some inadequacy on my part, I made a huge effort to get my message across, saying to Adela:

'Is anything wrong? I'm pretty tired and I could be expressing myself badly, but I had the impression from your letter that you realised I was in possession of vital evidence which would exonerate your husband. Naturally, I concluded that you wanted to find out if I was prepared to speak up, so I came to tell you that I am. It's as simple as that.'

'And I certainly do appreciate it, Theresa,' Adela said, rousing herself to speak at last, but still frowning in a way I found inexplicable. 'I really do, dear, but . . .'

'But what?'

'You see, my child, for us it is not so simple,' Dr Müller said. He had been hovering in the background during my speech, but now entered the group and sat down on the arm of the sofa. I thought he was going to place a hand on my shoulder, but he withdrew it, pushing it through his own springy grey hair instead, and went on, in the manner of one seeking the right words for an idiot:

'So, if we seem a little slow, you are asked to forgive us. I think I speak for all when I say we are now wondering how it is you should know in advance what we were going to ask you. Nothing of this has been mentioned in the press, or anywhere at all, except between ourselves. Is it possible that you have seen Sven, and he has told you, himself?'

'No, certainly not. I've been working all day and, besides, I don't even know where they've taken him.'

'So! Then may I ask how you should already know what we are speaking about?'

'Oh, for heaven's sake,' I said impatiently. 'What do you think? Isn't it obvious to a child of four that you want a statement about what I had seen, including the time and place?'

'Then, my dear young lady, I must congratulate you. Not only to have seen this thing, but to guess the importance, when nothing has been made public, that is quite something! Did she perhaps mention it, herself? Eh, yeh, yeh! Here we have our solution, I think.'

'Nothing of the kind. We are completely at cross-purposes, if you must know.'

To emphasise the point, I heaved myself upright, to the great annoyance of the poodle, who growled in a threatening way, before twisting himself back into a comfortable knot. 'Frankly, I have no idea what you are talking about. What do you mean and what is she supposed to have told me?'

'I knew it,' Adela said in a bored tone. 'I told you all along it was a waste of time.'

'But what is all this about?' I demanded. 'If I knew that, I could say my piece and then perhaps I could go home.'

Dr Müller took over again and this time he really did lay a hand briefly on my shoulder, saying with the utmost gravity:

'It is about a gold necklace.'

'Oh, that! What about it?'

'You knew that it was missing when . . . when our poor Leila was found?'

'Yes, it was in the papers.'

'But not that the police found it in Sven's possession and this is why he has been arrested?'

'No, I didn't know that, but the point is . . .'

'Forgive me, but no more confusions, please! The point is that the necklace was found here, in this apartment.'

'Found by the police?'

'Exactly. One of them was making a search, while another was in here, questioning Sven and Adela. They did this to all of us.'

'And where was it hidden?'

'Not hidden at all. Wrapped in some paper in his overcoat pocket.'

I certainly had to hand it to that policeman. Knowing something of Sven's eccentric ways, it was the obvious place to look, but for a stranger to have assessed him so accurately amounted to genius. However, this was not the sort of comment they expected of me, so I endeavoured to look suitably stunned.

'So! You are finding this hard to believe, but there is a quite simple explanation.'

'Which the police find hard to believe, I take it?'

'Yes, although it is not at all impossible. Simply that the clasp of this necklace, which is made like a snake's head, with a ruby and pearl, has been broken and so she cannot wear it.'

'You're not suggesting she gave it away, on that account?'

'No, no. It was something very precious to her. It had some good luck meaning, so she would wish always to wear it. But she had explained about the broken clasp to Sven, and he, who knows so many experts in so many different worlds, offered to take it to a jeweller of his acquaintance, where the repair could be done with very small expense and so delicately that she would not be able to see the difference.'

'Yes, from the little I know of him that sounds reasonable enough, but where do I come in?'

'I shall explain. When your cousin spoke to Jonathan on the telephone last night, she told him that you had actually met Leila in the morning and talked with her. They were quite excited about it, these young people, saying that you must have been one of the last to see her alive. Is it true?'

'That I was one of the last to see her alive? Of course not. It was only eleven o'clock in the morning when I met her.'

'But, you see, this may be very important. I should tell you that she left her house very early, before breakfast even. She was very conscientious and we think she had meant to get to her office before anyone was about, to catch up with all the work that had been neglected. We know that she was there, in fact, before nine o'clock, because that was when she met Sven and told him about the broken necklace. But she was very badly upset about this, and about other things as well, and so he told her he would get it mended for her, and he advised her not to worry so much about the work, but to go home and rest for a few days more.'

'But she didn't take his advice?'

'It seems not. From what we can trace, she must have spent the rest of the day wandering about on her own. We can find no one except yourself who saw her at all. So you see now how important it is to know whether she was wearing this necklace when you met her?'

'You mean, you are not even convinced, yourselves, that his story is true?' I glanced enquiringly at Reg Baker as I spoke, but his face was buried in his hands and I could not even be sure that he was listening. Adela answered for him:

'Oh sure, I believe it. It's just the kind of screwy thing that would happen to Sven, but apparently Leila didn't tell another soul, and who'll take my word? You're an outsider, with no reason to protect him, so that's different. If you don't remember, or if you have some idea she was wearing the necklace when you saw her, we'll forget the whole thing. That's why I wanted to see you privately, before we go to work on it with the lawyers.'

'Oh, I've no objection to co-operating with you over that,' I said brightly. 'To be candid, I don't remember whether she was wearing a necklace or not, but I'm quite prepared to say she was, to whom it may concern.'

This airy assurance was greeted with something less than jubilation. Dr Müller sighed, and then picked up my empty glass and walked away to refill it; and Reg Baker addressed me for the first time:

'I'm not saying you don't mean well, but it's no go.'

'What isn't?'

'Your swearing any old thing you reckon might help to whitewash Sven. They're no fools, these police geezers. They'd trip you up in no time, if you came out with a tale like that without being sure of your facts.'

'The point is,' I said grandly, taking a swig of my well-freshened drink, 'they'll forget all about necklaces when they hear what else I have to tell them.'

Once again, I had somehow struck the wrong note and the atmosphere seemed to grow even more leaden and hostile, although it may have been partly the heat and the alcohol which gave me the sensation of drowning in warm mud. I made another feeble attempt to oust the dog from my lap, but this woman/poodle relationship had got off on an unequal footing and there was no drawing back. This time there was a round of rumbling growls, before it bunched itself even tighter on my numbed thighs. Ignoring this, Adela said slowly:

'You have something else? Maybe you should tell us about it?'

'I was going to. It was my sole purpose in coming here. I happen to be in a unique position to assert positively that your husband is innocent.'

'Is that so? How do you figure that?'

'Because I saw him in a cinema, several miles from the scene of the crime, at the precise time when it must have been committed.'

This announcement really did set a cat among those quatre pigeons, although now there was an element of derision in their disbelief. Thea shook her head in a puzzled way and Adela said, smiling sadly:

'Oh no, no, Theresa. It's very dear of you, and I appreciate what you're trying to do, but it wouldn't be any use.'

'I'm not making it up, you know. It's the literal truth.' Once again, Dr Müller stepped into the breach and I got another therapeutic pat on the shoulder:

'No one is suggesting you made it up, but nevertheless it is impossible. Believe me, Sven cannot have been miles away in a cinema. He is known to have been at IDEAS at twenty past seven, and again at ten minutes to eight. Several people who know him well have seen him there.'

Rage and frustration boiled up inside me and, lashing out at the nearest target, I pushed impatiently at the poodle's hind quarters, so that it slithered forward and its head pitched down over my knees. Instantly, its body tautened like a steel spring, its lips drew back in a hideous grin and it began to tremble violently. Hoping to retrieve the situation I grabbed its collar, but at the first touch it whipped round like a cobra and took a slice out of my right hand.

It was almost a relief to let out a yell of pain and shock and I put as much energy into it as I could muster. It had them all on their feet and clustering round in no time. I fell back against the sofa and closed my eyes. Their faces bobbing round, so close to mine, questioning, commiserating, explaining, was more than I could stand and for a moment I truly believed I would faint.

Somebody removed the dog, Adela presumably, for I could hear her telling it that Mummie was not pleased, and I fancied it was Thea who calmly went to work with bandages and disinfectant. If so, she was remarkably deft and I felt nothing worse than a slight stiffness in my hand, although I did not bother to open my eyes and tell them so. They went on explaining things over and over again, but there was not an object or a person in the room that I wished to look at.

I had sent Pierre away, so the Müllers drove me home in the Mercedes. They were kind and patient, speaking in soft, reassuring voices, as we swept through the glistening deserted streets. Clearly, they were trying to impress on me their sincere belief that I had not invented my story, but that it was a straightforward case of mistaken identity. But I had heard it all before, in Adela's drawing-room, and I didn't pay much attention. One half of my mind was fixed on Robin's warning to have nothing further to do with these people; the other was asking how I should feel in six months' or a year's time, when I learnt that Sven Carlsen had been executed for crime he could not possibly have committed.

(iii)

They both escorted me to the lift, but I would not allow them to come any further, saying that I had my key. I could not be bothered to get it out, though, and leant against the top banister, praying that Ellen would not waste time reconnoitring through the spy-hole, as otherwise she was liable to witness something more sensational than she had bargained for.

As it happened, the door was flung open in a matter of seconds, and I was confronted by Robin, in a towering rage.

I was too thunderstruck and he, it appeared, too angry to speak, and we might have remained there for half an hour, doing our absurd mime, had not Ellen materialised and broken it up.

'There you are!' she said cheerfully. 'I explained to him how you sometimes have to work late. I told him you'd be all right, but he wouldn't listen.'

'All right?' Robin bellowed. 'She's not all right at all. And what has she done to her hand? Why is it all bandaged up like that?'

'Do you think I could come inside?' I said weakly. 'I'm rather tired, as it happens.'

They stood aside to let me pass, then both followed me into my bedroom, Robin still raging on:

'And, before you launch into one of your romances, I may as well warn you, Tessa, that I rang the studios two hours ago and they said you'd already left, so let's cut out that bit where you tell me you were kept on the set until ten o'clock.'

Since this feeble excuse was the only one which had so far occurred to me, there was nothing for it but to break into noisy sobs, which was not difficult to do and had a fairly magical effect. Ellen sped away to heat up some of the chalky liquid which the French call milk, Robin backed nervously on to the defensive and, as my own scalding emotions were blubbered away, I realised that the only sensible move was to acquaint him with all that had passed and to plant the responsibility for further action squarely on his shoulders. However, there were questions to be got through first.

'What are you doing here?' I asked, getting in first with these. 'And why didn't you let me know?'

'I tried to. God knows, I tried, but your telephone was engaged for two solid hours this morning.'

'There was a reason for that,' I assured him.

'I felt sure there would be.'

'I was trying to ring you.'

'Oh, were you? I confess that didn't occur to me. I concluded that you'd either gone to sleep with the receiver off, or were playing some crazy game of cops and robbers, all on your own. The second seemed the more probable, so I caught an early plane.'

'But you still haven't explained why you caught a plane at all.'

'Come to that, you haven't explained what you've been up to for the last couple of hours.'

'No, but I intend to. It's a long story, though, whereas yours must fit in a nutshell. Presumably, it was a last-minute whim, because you hadn't planned it when I spoke to you last night. Or had you?'

'No, but whim is the wrong word. In the language of the beat, I acted on information received.'

'From whom?'

'My colleague in the piscine. He telephoned me at eight o'clock this morning.'

'To tell you about Sven's arrest?'

'Among other things. I can't honestly say that the entente was quite so cordiale this morning. Possibly the fact that Carlsen had been run in for murder, within a week of my seeking information about him, carried a faint whiff of the perfide Albion, but I hope to have convinced him that it was sheer coincidence.'

'And did he tell you why Sven had been arrested?'

'He did, and I must say it sounded a bit thin to me. Specially in view of what you'd told me.'

'There are wheels within wheels.'

'Which you are now about to put in motion?'

'Just as soon as Ellen is in bed. This may take all night, but it doesn't matter because I feel quite bobbish again, now that you're here, and I'm not on call tomorrow; or Monday, either. The way I snarled things up for them today, it may well be that they need a couple of days to rewrite my part and cut out about eighty per cent of it, but I'll live through that tragedy when I come to it. First, I'm going to tell you all about a visit I've just paid to Adela Carlsen.'

When I had done so he said thoughtfully: 'Yes, it's a puzzle, I agree. Normally, I'd award you top marks in the observation test, but is it possible that you've slipped up this time? The alternative, that Sven has an identical twin running around in Paris, is something which I refuse even to contemplate.'

'So do I; mainly because someone would surely have seen fit to mention it. But it's so frustrating, Robin. If only Ellen had been standing where I was, I'm sure she'd have seen him, too.'

'But she didn't, so there's no point in wasting regrets over that. What was it about his appearance that chiefly struck you? His coat, for instance, and his special way of wearing it?'

'Partly that, I suppose; but also his hat half over his eyes and his head thrust forward. It makes him look like a tortoise standing on its hind legs.'

'They don't have any, but I know what you mean. Only it could be that these rather marked characteristics are awfully easy to imitate. Could someone have been impersonating him, by any chance?'

'But to what end? Presumably only to provide him with an alibi, which is the one thing it hasn't done. Besides, he did turn his head when I called out and only someone hearing his own name would have such quick reflexes.'

'Unfortunately, none of this disposes of the real snag.'

'Which is?'

'That, as far as I can make out, Sven himself doesn't claim to have been in the cinema that evening. Can you think of any single reason for that, except that he wasn't there?'

'I know that sounds logical,' I admitted, 'but there's something wrong somewhere. I'm sure I did see him, and everyone who says I didn't must be lying.'

'Well, that's been known, too; but just who are all these people?'

'Not so many, actually. In fact, it boils down to three; his secretary and two others.'

'Start with her.'

'Well, you know what she's like. A prim, middle-aged spinster, who probably lives a blameless life in some genteel suburb. She says he was working in his office when she left at twenty past seven, and I can't see any reason why she should be making it up.'

'Perhaps not, but does she normally stay as late as that?'

'No. Apparently, some people are there till eight or nine, and Sven is one of them; but they're mostly heads of departments. Most of the clerical staff knock off between half past five and six, but that particular evening happened to be the one when Mademoiselle Pêche has her weekly orgy in the staff supermarket. It's a kind of co-operative affair in the upper basement and it stays open until eight o'clock. Anyway, when Pêche had finished her rounds there, she went into the cafeteria, which is also on that floor, to take the weight off her feet and get a snack, before setting off to Meudon, or wherever it is; and there she met a friend.'

'So they got talking, as the saying goes?'

'And wound up arranging to spend the evening together. They were going to a concert and that's how Mademoiselle happened to trot upstairs to her office at seven-fifteen.'

'I don't follow you.'

'Well, you see, she'd lumbered herself with this great stack of groceries and wine and so on, and she didn't fancy carting it round the concert halls, so the idea was to leave it in her office overnight. When she got there, the communicating door to Sven's room was open and she could see him working at his desk.'

'Did he say anything?'

'Not as far as I know, but she knew he had a report to finish, which would take him a couple of hours, so there was no reason to disturb him. She just dumped the parcels and padded off to join her friend. Exit Miss Peach.'

'And enter who?'

'If we jump straight into Act Two, it's Enter Mrs Müller. There's a short scene in between, but I'll take that later, and you'll soon see why.'

'And what was her role?'

'She was the next to see him. She had been at a hair-dresser's in Avenue de Suffren and she came out of there at half past seven.'

'Sorry to keep raising the same eyebrows, but wasn't that rather late?'

'Oh, not for Paris, Robin. It's quite acceptable to book an appointment for six in the evening, and they sometimes

leave you under the dryer for ages, if twenty other customers happen to roll up without any appointment at all. She
obviously hadn't counted on getting out even as early as
that, because she'd arranged to pick up her husband at his
office at eight o'clock. It was only ten minutes' walk from
the hairdresser's, so she took it slowly.'

'Including a stroll through the Champ de Mars, by any
chance?'

'Oddly enough, yes. She made no secret of it, but she says
she went across the top end, near the Eiffel Tower, which
in fact would have been her direct route. Mrs Baker was
found at the southern end, not far from the Joffre statue.'

'And she saw nothing?'

'So she says. Her part in the plot begins when she got
to IDEAS. It was still not quite eight, but the receptionists
had left and she didn't want to risk taking the lift up, in case
she crossed with her husband coming down, so she sat on
one of those leather couches to wait for him. When she'd
been there about five minutes, a lift stopped at the ground
floor and out stepped Sven. He'd got his hat and coat on
and he walked past and out by the main door. Apparently,
he normally travels to work by Métro, because Adela mostly
has the car, so it was all according to routine. He says he
arrived home about eight-thirty, but Adela and Jonathan
were both out, so that's just his word.'

'How about Adela? What was she doing?'

'She'd been playing bridge, but she left the party early
because she had an appointment with someone called Marie
Claire, who runs a dogs' beauty parlour, somewhere in
Montmartre. The traffic through the centre of Paris was so
terrible that it took her over an hour to get home and she
arrived there a few minutes after Sven. Anyway, if he did
get back at eight-thirty, that's just about the time it would

have taken him to get from the office; or, to look at it another way, from the cinema.'

'And I'm even more in the dark as to why he has been arrested.'

'At this point, so was everyone else, but unfortunately there's this small scene between Acts One and Two, which hadn't been made known when Mrs Müller and Miss Pêche told their bit. Reg Baker gave it away, unintentionally, not having heard what they'd said.'

'Gave what away?'

'What he saw in the car park, in the lower basement. He was questioned about his own movements, naturally, and he said that at a quarter to eight he brought the lift down and walked across to his car. So, of course, they asked for proof and, not knowing any better, he said he was sure Carlsen would confirm it, because he'd caught sight of him by one of the other cars and had called out goodnight. He hadn't stopped to chat or anything, because he was collecting his wife from some gathering of the gurus and he was pushed for time. It was when he found that she'd never turned up for it and wasn't at home when he got back there, either, that he rang the police.'

'Just like that?'

'How do you mean?'

'I mean, he didn't ring round to any of their friends first, or ask the neighbours if they'd seen her? He was a bit precipitate about bringing the police in, wasn't he? Unless he had good reason to know there was something wrong?'

'Well, they haven't been in Paris very long, so perhaps they weren't on those terms with the neighbours. And she'd been acting a bit strangely, to put it mildly, so it wasn't quite so peculiar as it sounds. But I'll tell you all about that some other time. I want you to hear about these stories they all told while they're still fresh in my mind. Then you can sift through them and decide who's lying and what we ought to do about it.'

'I'm afraid your blind faith is somewhat misplaced, but go on.'

'Well, it was because he rang the police that they were able to identify her. Up to then, they hadn't even known who she was, because her bag hadn't been found.'

'Has that turned up, by the way?'

'I don't think so, but I can't see that it signifies, one way or the other. I doubt if she often carried one. But you see what all this means, Robin? If Sven was really in the car park between twenty and ten to eight, then he can't have been in his office, as he says.'

'Whereas, he could easily have just come from the Champ de Mars?'

'Precisely. If he'd gone down to the lower basement as soon as his secretary had dumped her parcels, he could have walked up the ramp to the street, crossed over and entered the Champ de Mars all in the space of about five minutes. Allow another five to get to the spot where he's presumed to have had an appointment with Leila Baker, and what have you got? All he had to do was clout her over the head, finish the job by strangling her and return to IDEAS by the same route, having picked up the necklace, which had got broken in the struggle, and stuffed it into his pocket, along with the weapon. All that remained was to get back into the lift and bring it up to the ground floor.'

'Where he came face to face with Mrs Müller?'

'Who naturally assumed that he had come down from his office. And it was sheer fluke that she was there at all. She's not even sure that he noticed her.'

'Incidentally, didn't it strike Baker as peculiar that Sven should be in the car park at all, since he was known to travel by Metro?'

'I don't think so. If he's speaking the truth, I suppose he assumed that he was getting a lift with someone else. Probably that did happen from time to time.'

'But Sven denies that he had made any such arrangement on this particular evening?'

'He denies everything. He says he left his office when the report was finished, took the lift to the ground floor, walked out of the building and went straight home.'

'And there's only Baker's word for it that he didn't do just that. It's pretty flimsy, because he admits that they didn't exchange any words. I realise that Carlsen's appearance is fairly distinctive, but the light down there is very dim and surely there's a strong possibility that he could have been mistaken?'

'There is worse to come,' I admitted.

'I thought there must be. Like forgetting to dispose of the weapon, for instance?'

'Oh, Robin! How on earth did you guess?'

'But I didn't, honestly. I was just being funny. You can't seriously mean . . . ?'

'Not quite as bad as that, but they've found the spanner they think was used to knock her out and he admits that it's one from his own tool kit. Furthermore, it had been dumped on the exact spot where Reg Baker claims to have seen him, in the car park.'

'That's right. I suppose, to a simple person, it might have seemed a natural place for it.'

'And do you consider Carlsen to be as simple as all that?'

'No,' I agreed, 'but my opinion isn't going to help him very much.'

'Specially if this spanner was covered with his prints, which I suppose is the next bit of news you've got for me?'

'No, it had been wiped, although not very efficiently. There were traces of blood and hair. I gather that the police haven't actually stated that these came from the scalp of Mrs Baker, but I expect they want to keep a few surprises up their sleeve.'

Robin was silent for a while, and then he said: 'Do you know, I can hardly recall a case of murder where the principal suspect appears to have behaved in a more moronic fashion? He must either be an arrogant fool, or else . . .'

'Or else someone is perjuring himself, knowing that for some reason Sven will keep quiet.'

'How did you interpret Baker's reactions this evening? On the face of it, he has the best motive of anyone. That is, if we're right about there being something between him and Adela. Although, you know, Tessa, we haven't really much to go on there. One overlooked conversation is hardly evidence of adultery. They could have been talking quite innocently.'

'Except that you and I both gained a quite different impression.'

'All the same, it would be nice to have a little more substance for it.'

'There's always Milly Carpenter,' I suggested.

'Milly Carpenter? Who's she?'

'Adela's dear friend in London, who she used to go and stay with so regularly, but doesn't any more. Adela couldn't wait to find out if I knew her, so she could have been the one to provide the alibi on all those London trips.'

'I don't see the connection.'

'Neither did I, until I discovered that her white-haired boy friend was Reg Baker, but there's a funny coincidence about that, because he used to work in London. Adela says she had to cut out her cross-Channel trips when they got the dogs, but it coincided very neatly with Reg being posted to Paris.'

'I see!'

'What's more, those two mixed-up poodles are supposed to rule her life and she certainly makes them an excuse for being away from home for long stretches; but when you see her with them she doesn't show any particular affection for them, nor they for her. It's other people, even strangers like myself, that they pester. So I should never be surprised if the dogs had become the Milly Carpenter of Paris.'

'Well, well! I wonder if you're right?'

'Unfortunately, even if I am, she can't have conspired with her Reginald to dispose of his wife, because he's completely in the clear. When he left his office he had a drink in the top floor bar with two other men, and they both remember what time he left.'

'Yes, no doubt; but what's ten minutes here or there between colleagues drinking together?'

'Nothing in the ordinary way, but he was fidgeting about collecting his wife from the swami, so the time was impressed on them.'

'Which isn't necessarily as innocent as it sounds. However, one thing begins to be clear.'

'I'm so glad. Do tell me what it is.'

'If Adela is speaking the truth, one can see why she was so bent on getting your evidence about the necklace. So far as I can see, no one has come up with Sven's motive, so if his story about the necklace turns out to be genuine, the whole case against him might begin to topple. Can't you shut your eyes and do some total recall?'

'No, it's no use. In the ordinary way, I think I might have noticed, but I was watching out for the car and I hardly

looked at her. Also, you know, Robin, there was something faintly repellent about that way she had of touching
one and pushing her face up so close. One tended to avert
one's eyes and pretend it wasn't happening. Anyway, I still
say it's irrelevant. I don't know how Sven came to have the
necklace in his pocket, but I do know that he couldn't have
been anywhere near the Champ de Mars between seven-
thirty and eight.'

'And, if you're as positive as all that, I'd be inclined to
go along with you. Let's hope, for Sven's sake, that we can
manage to persuade a few other people as well. I'll drop the
word, but that's about all I can do; and you, Tessa, must
now pipe down and shut up about it.'

'Oh, why do you say that?'

'Because, my love, if there is a conspiracy, or if one of
these people is giving false evidence to cover his own tracks,
we all know who might be in a position to trip him up. It
would be safer all round if you would allow them to believe
that you're now quite satisfied that you were mistaken about
seeing Sven in the cinema. I hope you didn't press the point
too much?'

'No, I felt too dazed and buffeted to utter a word.'

'That's good, because we don't want anyone to get the
idea that you might be a danger to him. You know what they
say about murderers in this part of the world?'

'No, what?'

'Il n'y a que le premier pas qui coûte.'

EIGHT

(i)

True to life's inexorable pattern, I woke early the next morning and, having no need to get up, found myself unable to slide back to sleep again.

It was too early for *Figaro*, so I decided to glance through the scripts which my agent had thrust into my hands at Heathrow. Moving stealthily, so as not to disturb Robin, I took down the red suitcase, eased out a pillow which he wasn't really using, and propped myself up for a comfortable and constructive period of study.

There were three typescripts and two were by authors whose names were familiar. Both these had been clipped into the regulation orange cover, which was my agent's trade mark, with the name and address of her offices prominently featured, along with stern injunctions relating to copyright, etcetera. The third one was much shorter, more of an outline scenario than a full-scale script. It consisted of about fifty rather carelessly typed pages, enclosed in an ordinary brown folder, and it occurred to me that it might have arrived too late to be put through the usual mill, but had nevertheless been considered promising enough to warrant immediate attention. I therefore started with this one.

Page One was headed: 'The Waiting Room', By Henry Fitzgerald, who was a new one on me, and in the pleasurable anticipation of setting some undiscovered genius on the first, or at any rate second rung to fame, I began to read.

It is tempting to pretend that the excitement of discovery grew dizzier with every word and that I very soon became lost in the imaginary world of H. Fitzgerald, Esq., but it would not be true. It was a spy story, not without merit, but melodramatic beyond all bounds. The setting was a remote, mountainous region of Southern Europe and the Waiting Room of the title was attached to a high-class private nut-house, most of whose patients suffered from delusions of having been wrongfully incarcerated.

An exception to this persecution mania was the hero, Simon Charrington. He, it soon became clear, really had been wrongfully incarcerated, through the machinations of an international spy group; and in order to outwit them he went into the full mad scene whenever a doctor or nurse hove in sight.

The story contained some imaginative twists and one or two scenes which I could envisage being very suspensefully worked out in the shooting, but I was at a loss to know why my agent had included it. Whereas the leading man's part provided unlimited scope for cat tearing, the only female role of any substance was that of a rather tiresomely mysterious nurse. This character, apart from prowling round the wards in a furtive manner when the patients were at lunch, was also the mistress of the head psychiatrist, one Felix Marcus, who was the villain of the piece and an important cog in the espionage machine. As the story developed, she gave indications of transferring her affections to the pseudo-demented hero, although whether because her feelings were engaged, or in order to engineer his downfall, remained in doubt.

Moreover, before I had even reached the halfway mark a sense of déjà vu had begun to intrude. I could not pin it down, and yet it was strong enough to suggest that this might be a treatment based on some novel which I had long ago read, or even a film which I had long ago seen.

I had half a mind to telephone my agent and interrogate her on these matters, but memories of my previous experience with the French telephone system stayed my hand. Furthermore, the craving for coffee and rolls had become so acute that I was prepared to make the supreme sacrifice of going in search of them, in person.

I could have saved myself the trouble, because Ellen was already in the kitchen, surrounded by dainty trays.

'Have we had enough spy stories?' I asked her. 'Or could we do with just one more?'

'Depends who played the spy. How's your hand?'

'Fair. It's God's mercy that I'm not on call for the next few days. The continuity girl would resign on the spot if she saw this bandage. Come to think of it, it's just as well I'm not the continuity girl. I daresay it will be weeks before I can hold a pen. How did your lunch go, by the way?'

'Pretty dreary, actually.'

'Oh why? Didn't Lupe do a good job?'

'She was okay, but Jono never stops talking about himself.'

'That can happen,' I admitted. 'One trains oneself to take it as a compliment. They don't all grow out of it.'

'He's got this fantastic Oedipus thing, too. I hope he grows out of that.'

'Oh, bound to, but you do surprise me. The only time I saw them together they didn't seem particularly chummy.'

'It's a love-hate relationship,' she explained, tipping coffee beans into the electric grinder. 'He's thought of everything.'

Some of the beans cascaded on to the floor and she scooped them up and flung them into the machine.

'They say that ninety per cent of our coffee is dust nowadays,' she explained.

'Whereas ninety per cent of our dust is coffee, I suppose? How about the stepfather relationship?'

'Oh, that's hate-hate.'

'Really? Jealousy and so forth?'

'Yes, and he blames him for breaking up his parents' marriage. And he says it's having to live in Paris which has changed his mother. She used to be dead keen about the home and do lots of committees and things. She was about the best known woman in their entire neighbourhood.'

'Where was that?'

'In New York, somewhere. And they had a fabulous house at Cape Cod, too, with ice dispensers on every floor. Jono would much rather spend his vacations there than in Paris. He has his own car at home, too, but he's not allowed to drive in France. They have four cars altogether. Imagine Mrs Carlsen giving all that up for silly old Sven!'

'Perhaps she was secretly bored by the home and the committees and only did them from a sense of duty. No one has a sense of duty in France.'

'Not Mr Carlsen, anyway. Jono says he's madly unfaithful. Always having sordid little affairs.'

'Now, how could he possibly know that?'

'Because he keeps tabs on him.'

'My goodness, that boy is a case, isn't he? Is it all dreamville, or does he really know what he's talking about?'

'A bit of both, I should think,' she replied, pouring boiling water over the coffee.

'Do you suppose he dislikes Sven enough to want to put a real spanner in the works?'

'What kind of spanner?'

'Oh, I didn't mean that literally,' I said hastily, 'I just meant spreading tales around which weren't strictly true.'

'Could be. He doesn't seem bothered about him being arrested. We plan to go skating today, by the way. Is that okay?'

'Can either of you skate?'

'Well, I'm not much good, but Jono's bound to be. His father was in the Olympic team.'

'Fancy that! Does Adela know that he takes you out?'

'Oh sure. She doesn't care. All she wants is not to have him around too much. She rang up his father last night and said he ought to go back to America, because it wasn't suitable for him to be here with all this fuss going on. I think it was just an excuse to get rid of him, actually.'

'And did it succeed?'

'No. His father said he was going on a trip somewhere, so it wouldn't be convenient. Jono says he's really going to Washington to advise the President, but nobody's supposed to know. Anyway, why are you so quizzy?'

'I've told you; I feel responsible.'

'Is that all? I thought maybe Robin was going to take a hand in the case, after all, and you thought it might be a good idea to find out a few things.'

'Unfortunately not. It's a pity, because then he could stay over for a bit, but he will keep insisting that it's no concern of his.'

Robin was not visible when I carried his tray in, but I could hear him splashing about under the shower. Since the bathroom had been designed to accommodate only one person, and then only when perpendicular, I swaddled the coffee pot in an eiderdown and began plastering my face with dewy moisturised démaquillage. In a few moments he emerged and studied the effect critically:

'Very weird! How about getting your hair done this morning?'

'Why would I bother to do that, when I can get it done for nothing at the studios?'

'But you said you wouldn't be going there until Tuesday, and if we mean to do the town this weekend you might want to look your best.'

'If you really think it's necessary . . .' I said doubtfully.

'You could telephone that well-turned-out Mrs Müller and ask her which one she goes to.'

'It so happens that I know which one she goes to,' I said, rounding on him in amazement. 'She pointed it out when they drove us back from lunch.'

'There you are, then! No trouble at all.'

'And what about you, pray? Another round of courtesy calls?'

'Among other things. Let's meet back here, shall we? We may have some notes to compare.'

One way and another, I was beginning to believe that if they handed me a stick labelled 'This Way Up' I should still grasp it by the wrong end.

(ii)

Mireille was the name of the assistant who ministered to Madame Müller and by some unprecedented miracle of chance she was disengaged and able to begin on me at once.

I think this must have been bending the truth a little because, although they peeled off my jacket, tipped me backwards over the basin and doused my head with water, as though there was not a minute to lose, it was practically bone dry again by the time Mireille teetered up to begin on stage two.

She upset a bottle of blue lotion over me and consulted my wishes as to the style of the coiffure. This presented no problems because, as I had foreseen, her English was remarkably good. When we had mapped out the design, I asked if Madame Müller had been coming to her for a long time. She scuffled about among the tools of her trade for a bit and then said:

'Some months, I think. Do you prefer the big rollers?'

'Yes, if you like. But she doesn't live around here, does she?'

'No. The sides coming forward? A little bit over the face, like this?'

'Yes, that's fine. I think they live in the seizième, so it must be quite a way for her to come.'

'I don't know. I think maybe her husband has his office somewhere in the quartier. That would make it convenient. It would be better to have some cut, next time.'

'Yes, I will. And that reminds me. Could you give Mrs Müller a message when she comes this afternoon? I forgot to . . .'

'She will not be here this afternoon. I am sorry, madame.'

'Are you sure? I thought Saturday was her day?'

'No, Wednesday. Every Wednesday when she can be in Paris. Would you like to come under the dryer?'

I consented and she slammed the hood down over my head, handed me some battered copies of *Paris-Match* and tripped away.

Madame Stéfane was more forthcoming, though not so hot with the English. We ran into our first misunderstanding while I was struggling with my purse and she asked if my hand had been blessed. However, she was so uproariously amused to discover that blessé was not one of those words which can be transposed phonetically into English that we became very chummy and she gave me an unlooked-for lead by saying how recognising she was for Madame Müller's recommendations.

'Oh, but her hair always looks so marvellous,' I gushed.

'But madame also has beautiful hairs,' Stéfane replied dutifully. 'Did she find her bag, the poor?'

'Whose bag?' I asked sharply.

'Madame Müller. She is so much deceived to find she is not leaving it here. We are searching upside down, as you may imagine, Madame, but everyone ignored it.'

This was strange, indeed, and I asked again: 'Her own bag, did you say?'

'But yes, madame.'

Mireille trotted up and applied herself fussily to the appointments book. Whipping through the pages, she gabbled away in an undertone to her employer. Among the few words I could catch was 'sac', which made sense to me, although I had a faint impression that it was not intended to.

I was formulating a new question when Mireille looked up with a dazzling smile and said how much she longed for the pleasure to see me again. She then held the door open for me to pass through and slammed it shut when I had reluctantly done so.

(iii)

'So I regret to tell you that is the one single note I have for comparison,' I confessed to Robin, who had arrived home a few minutes ahead of me. 'And what a note! Admittedly, my extensive knowledge of French informs me that for "deceived" one should read "disappointed", but such a mild reaction makes it all the more mysterious. Imagine being merely disappointed to find that you'd come out without your bag! One would be more likely to leave one's head at home.'

'And yet you took it in your stride that Mrs Baker should be abroad without hers.'

'That's different. For one thing, she could obviously conceal a dozen pockets and pouches inside all those layers of sari. Also she seems to have been devoid of personal vanity; but Mrs Müller is the type who wouldn't move a yard without a battery of make-up within reach. I daresay she could have carried essentials like her purse and keys in a coat pocket, but what about all the other junk one needs a bag for?'

'So what construction do you put on it?'

'I simply don't know, Robin, unless she'd left it in the car or something. The only certainty is that she did keep her regular six o'clock appointment last Wednesday and from personal experience of their methods she wouldn't have got away much before seven-thirty. Searching around for the bag would have meant even more delay.'

'Unless, of course, that was simply a device to impress the time on everyone.'

'I thought of that, naturally, but it's so far-fetched. If she had purposely dropped a glove or something one could understand it, but a bag is not a thing one could pretend about. Either she was carrying one, or she wasn't. They're not easy to conceal.'

'Specially if they happen to contain very large spanners?'

'Exactly. She would not only have had to carry the spanner quite openly to the Champ de Mars and bash her friend over the head with it; she would then need to carry it quite openly, and covered with bloodstains, all the way to IDEAS, to dump it in the car park. It's just not possible.'

'Except that it occurs to me, Tessa, that she could have had some kind of shopping bag, which would have served the purpose even better.'

I shook my head: 'Madame Stéfane told me they'd searched the place upside down, and I don't doubt she meant exactly that. She and Mireille are very tough nuts and I can't see them being satisfied with any search which didn't include shopping bags or any other container which she might have been carrying.'

'So your note does seem to have been worth comparing, after all. You're sure you've got it straight, though? I hate to imply that your French is less than perfect, but could you possibly have misunderstood?'

'Not possibly,' I said. 'And just in case you still doubt me I had better admit that we were speaking English. But if I might put a question of my own, why this fantastic interest? I thought you said this was a local affair and no concern of yours?'

'One can't repress a faint curiosity.'

'Even to the point of pushing me off to the hairdresser's to check on Thea Müller's alibi?'

'Well, it was harmless enough and your hair wasn't looking all that hot. I didn't really expect anything to come of it, because the police have doubtless checked it, too. That may be why Mireille was a bit clam-like.'

'Why don't you ask?'

'Ask who what?'

'Whether they've checked her alibi. And don't look so innocent, Robin. I know perfectly well this isn't just personal curiosity, whatever you may pretend. You've already hinted that you didn't come prancing over here just because my telephone was engaged. In fact, the only unpremeditated bit was catching an earlier plane, wasn't it?'

'But it had nothing to do with Mrs Baker's death. At least, only indirectly.'

'What does that mean?'

'Simply that it's true that I was coming anyway, but on a different job. On the other hand, the murder might conceivably have some part in the general scheme of things, if you follow me.'

'In other words, there could be some connection with the espionage thing?'

'It's possible, but in the meantime, acting on information I received from this side of the Channel, I've been following up some leads and there may well be some links in this particular chain right in our own backyard.'

'You don't say?'

'So I am authorised to come here and report, as and when necessary.'

'I couldn't be more delighted.'

'Well, that's as it should be, because it's mainly on your account that I can come and go so openly. You have provided me with the best possible excuse for the occasional weekend in Paris.'

'So even if the film turns out to be a record-breaking flop I shall feel I have done my bit for democracy, which will be some consolation. What's the set-up, or can't you tell me?'

'Well, you've heard that there's this little tiny branch of IDEAS in London. It was formed as a kind of liaison office and also for recruiting staff from England and the Commonwealth, although it's run, I need hardly add, by an international team. They don't get half the same privileges as the people in Paris, mainly because the level of jobs is much lower; but they operate on rather the same lines as a foreign consulate, and naturally there's a good deal of coming and going between the two countries.'

'Sven was doing some coming and going, when we first met him,' I suggested.

'Yes, but one can't attach much significance to that. I imagine it's fairly routine.'

'The only novelty on that occasion being his prankish behaviour with my suitcase. Oh goodness, Robin, can that be the answer? Do you suppose he used it to smuggle in the secret plans?'

'Why should he bother, when he only had to tuck them in his own brief-case? In the unlikely event of a customs man asking him to open it, he would only have been looking for contraband watches or cameras.'

'Unless, by any chance, they had been tipped off about him?'

Robin shook his head: 'No good. It's a lovely idea, but my old boy told me categorically that they'd never even heard of Carlsen.'

'But Sven may not know that. He might have got the wind up, for some reason. Whereas, if they'd opened my case and found suspicious-looking documents, he only had to let out a scream that he'd picked up the wrong case by mistake.'

'Leaving you to march off with the loot?'

'Oh, he'd have cooked up some story to get it back, you may be sure. No one could accuse him of lack of inventiveness, and we mustn't forget that all of it happened before he found out you were a copper. Honestly, Robin, I do think this could account for so much.'

'Not for everything, though. It wouldn't explain his cutting you dead in the cinema.'

I considered this and then said tentatively: 'Are you sure it wouldn't? I expect you'll say I'm trying to twist the facts to prove my point, but supposing he'd been there on some spying job? Mightn't that have induced him to keep quiet about it, even at the cost of being arrested for something he hadn't done? He might bank on further evidence coming to light to get him off the murder hook, even before he came to trial. Whereas, if the cinema had been the meeting-place with another operator in the spy ring, he couldn't possibly produce it as an alibi. It might get him into far more serious trouble, not only with the police, but also with the people he was working for. For all we know, it may be loyalty to them which is keeping him so quiet; but I should think it's more likely that he's caught between two fires and is gambling on the fact that ultimately he's less likely to get burned by the murder charge than by the other thing.'

'There's some logic in that,' Robin admitted. 'The trouble is that he has no known record. But still, you could say that of some of the most successful spies in the business, couldn't you? Perhaps it would be worth while to contact the Danish authorities, after all. Some little item might turn up.'

'And, while you're about it, you could check on his activities in the States. He told me he was posted there for several years, which is how he met Adela. We might get Toby to dig something up. He knows masses of people in New York and it would amuse him.'

'I would just as soon he found something else to amuse himself with, if you don't mind. The whole story, with bangles and bells on, would be round New York in a week.'

'What's our next move, then? Perhaps you'd like me to go out and buy myself a poodle? Then I could take it over to Marie Claire for a shampoo and set?'

'No, one at a time. Let's leave Adela till Monday. Why don't we just go out and look about us? We haven't even been up the Eiffel Tower yet, have we?'

'No, we haven't, have we?'

'We ought to do that before they take it away to make room for another car park. And we might try that restaurant across the road for lunch?'

'Oh, not that one, please, Robin.'

'Why? What's wrong with it?'

'Nothing, as far as I know, but it's where Mademoiselle Pêche goes for her hot chocolate. I'm always seeing her.'

'Well, why shouldn't she, poor old girl?'

'No reason. I just don't want to be there, if she should turn up. She's so damn ladylike, for one thing, and I'm sure she's got a terrific crush on Sven. It would make me feel guilty to be enjoying myself while she suffered. Let's just go to our usual place. It's in the right direction for the Eiffel Tower.'

'Very well. And how about a stroll afterwards, through those Martian Fields?'

(iv)

'You do realise we're walking in the wrong direction?' I asked, an hour or two later.

We had entered the Champ de Mars from the Avenue Joseph Bouvard and, after passing through the semi-enclosed shrubbery where Mrs Baker had been found, had wheeled left and struck out into open territory, towards the Avenue Bourdonnais.

'Yes, but I think I'd prefer to visit the Invalides instead,' Robin replied. 'An equally impressive building in its way, and that lunch has made me disinclined for heights.'

The Maréchal glared over our heads from his pinnacle on our right, and behind him was the Ecole Militaire, the hands on its clock pointing, as we drew level, to ten to three. Robin had checked his watch when we left the Avenue Suffren and I asked him how long the journey had taken, so far.

'Just on ten minutes. A bit tight, isn't it?'

'With another half mile to go, by my reckoning. Allowing a stop of at least five minutes on the way, I don't see how she could have covered it in less than twenty, even if she'd kept up your pace, which would have been a miracle in itself.'

'She's a more athletic type than you, don't forget. And cheer up; I know a nice café on the corner, not far from here. If you're very good, I'll allow you a ten-minute coffee break.'

'What drives you on in this inexorable fashion?' I asked, flopping into a chair. The pavement tables were all taken, so we had chosen one inside, as near the window as we could get. 'I thought we had already disposed of Thea?'

'Keep your voice down, could you? We're not a hundred miles from a certain organisation and I have no doubt that various members of it frequent this café.'

'Not on Saturday afternoon, and you haven't answered my question.'

'No harm in making a thorough job of it. I agree that no one in his right mind would carry a spanner through Paris in broad daylight, having just used it to commit murder, but it's just as well to get the time element sorted out, as well.'

'What I don't understand is your reason for making a thorough job of it at all.'

'Force of habit, I suppose.' He paused, and after a moment went on: 'No, it isn't only that, Tessa. The truth is, I'm a bit hung up on this business of your seeing a certain party at the cinema. You're still sure of that, by the way? No second thoughts?'

'None.'

'No, and that's what bothers me. I mentioned it at our meeting this morning. They didn't exactly laugh in my face, but it was touch and go. All of which is perfectly understandable, from their point of view, and yet, as you've pointed out, he could be concealing something which he'd rather face a murder charge than have brought to light.'

'Which means that all the others are lying, too?'

'One may be; not necessarily all of them.'

'So who's next on your list? Adela, I suppose? What do we say to that story about it taking her an hour to get home from Montmartre? It's a bit steep, isn't it? On the other hand, Adela seems to be the only one who is lifting a finger to clear him. It was she who convened the conference about the necklace.'

'There is no guarantee that she expected, or even wished you to come up with the right answer. If she knows more about the necklace than she pretended, she may have wanted to use you to get Sven in even deeper.'

'Oh, Robin, could any woman be such a monster?' I asked, a movement at the table just beyond the plate-glass division causing me to glance up as I spoke. Three people had stood up to leave and someone else had snatched the table before they had finished collecting their belongings. The window was sound-proof, so I continued in an ordinary tone: 'You were right about one thing, though. One of them does come here on Saturday afternoon.'

'Which one?'

I gestured with my glass: 'Him with the newspaper. He's got his back to us now, but there's no mistaking that head.'

'Has he spotted us?'

'I don't think so.'

'We don't want to draw attention to ourselves, so you'd better stay here and get the bill, in case the waiter thinks we're welshing.'

'Where are you going?'

'Not far. Stay here until you've paid for the coffee and then follow me round. It'll look less contrived if I go in first.'

He got up, moving his chair very quietly, and walked towards the interior of the café. Then he turned and made for the side entrance into Avenue Motte Piquet, and I saw him pause for a minute at the newspaper stall on the corner.

Then, *Times* in hand, he came on round again, an anxious searching look on his face, the very picture, as he no doubt fondly imagined, of the harassed British tourist clutching his talisman of sanity in a demented foreign world. The act continued as he drew level, stopped to scan the crowd on the pavement and, with a delighted start of surprise, lo and behold! espied a table with only one occupant.

It was just about the most overdone performance I had ever witnessed, but at least it had the effect of attracting the startled attention of approximately sixteen people, including the one for whose benefit it had all been designed. Mr Baker looked up.

I could see his face in profile and it did not look particularly cordial, but Robin can be very thick-skinned when he chooses. He had rested both hands on the back of a chair and was talking earnestly, using the shy, diffident approach, and getting absolutely nowhere. Mr Baker's responses were confined to an occasional nod and his eyes continually strayed back to his newspaper. At one point, still without looking up, he shook his head firmly, which could have meant that he had no objection to this stranger sharing his table, but could also have meant the exact opposite, and I decided it was time to intervene.

I wrapped a five-franc note round the bill, tucked it under the saucer and collected my bag and gloves. Then I swung open the door and, smiling brightly, tapped Robin on the shoulder:

'Sorry I'm so terribly late, darling, but honestly, the Paris traffic . . . Oh, Mr Baker! I didn't see you. Have you two already met, then? This is Reg Baker, Robin, a friend of the Carlsens. You remember my telling you . . . I say, would you mind terribly if we sat here until there's a free table?'

'It's a free country, so they tell me,' Mr Baker said not very graciously. 'But I'm not promising you'll find me very good company.'

I said eagerly: 'No, please. We don't want to thrust ourselves on you. It's just that there's not much room at the moment and all this tramping around makes one feel so absolutely dead; but don't bother about us if you'd rather just sit and read your paper.'

He showed every indication of taking me at my word and Robin said:

'All the same, if I may . . . Well, that is, Tessa's told me about this tragic affair, and I hope you won't mind my saying that you have our deepest sympathy?'

'Thanks. I'll take it as read, if you've no objection. What are you doing in this neck of the woods, anyway? Thought you'd taken off days ago?'

'Just back for the weekend. Tell me: what news of Carlsen? I heard about his arrest, but is there no chance of some mistake there?'

'Shoulda thought you'd know better, Price, than to ask a question like that.'

'Forgive me, but I speak as a friend of theirs. This is not my patch and I'm free to express normal sentiments.'

'Of curiosity?'

Robin remained smooth as velvet: 'Of concern, rather. I was thinking that if anything could make matters even more intolerable it might be the knowledge that one of your own friends was responsible.'

'Then you and I don't see things alike, chum. If Carlsen's responsible, as you put it, the only thing that could make it worse would be him getting off scot-free. Far as I'm concerned, it's up to the police to decide whether he's guilty or not, and if he is I hope he fries, that's all.'

'But what about his wife?'

'What about her?' Mr Baker asked in an even more offensive tone.

'Whatever your opinion of him, I suppose you're not indifferent to her feelings?'

'Hell, no. I'm not that vindictive, I hope.'

'I'm glad, because I was going to ask your advice. I know very little of these people, except that they befriended us, as strangers within their gates, so to speak, and I'd like to send a word of sympathy, if I could. It's an awkward situation because I don't know Mrs Carlsen well enough to be sure how she would feel about letters and so on; but Tessa and I both thought there might be something we could do for her, in a practical way. Perhaps you could tell her that for me?'

I was rather impressed by the quiet dignity of this utterance, despite the suspicion that there was something of a quiet craftiness in it, too; but it had the effect of literally inflaming Mr Baker and two red spots of anger showed up on his pallid face.

'Now, look here, chum, let's get this straight, right off. When I said I wasn't vindictive, I meant just that and no more. Get it? I don't know how you people would react in a situation like this; keep the stiff upper lip in place, maybe, but you won't catch me hanging around Adela and carrying messages. Daresay that'd be the correct thing in your part of the world, but it's not for me. Personally, I'm uncouth and I'd find it highly embarrassing to be with Adela just now. Oh, I know I was in her apartment the other evening,' he went on, fixing me with an accusing stare, 'but she roped me into that council of war before I'd even picked myself up off the floor. You may have noticed that I didn't have too much to contribute to the discussions. If you want it straight, I was pretty well out on my feet, but I heard enough of what went on not to want a repetition. So my advice is, if you've got anything to say to Adela, go ahead and say it, but count me out.'

I was rather floored by this heavy dose of the rough-diamond, plain-speaking treatment, but Robin coolly pretended to be impressed:

'When you put it like that, I do understand. Awful, isn't it, how one falls into this trap of only seeing things from one's own point of view? In a way, I suppose the most tactful thing might be for mere acquaintances like ourselves to keep out of it? Presumably, she has plenty of real friends who will rally round, even though she is a foreigner?'

'And her son, you know,' I reminded him in a sugary voice, joining in the act. 'He must be some comfort, even though he is so young.'

There was no satisfying Mr Baker, though, and these syrupy observations only produced a snort of disgust:

'Think so? If you ask me, a spoilt brat like that'd be more trouble than enough. She'd have shipped him back, if she could, but it seems his Dad don't want him, either. Can't say I blame him.'

I do not believe I would have let out a squeal of astonishment at this point, but Robin was taking no chances. He gave me a sharp kick under the table, with the result that I let out a squeal of astonishment.

Stifling it quickly, I said: 'Is that so? Poor boy! How horrid not to be wanted by either of them! After all, if he is spoilt, it could be partly their fault; or do you blame that on Sven, too?'

The most objectionable thing about French waiters is their rigid code of honour. There I was, eagerly probing away, and getting results, too, when the indoor waiter had to come tumbling out and upset the apple-cart all over our table. There was only two francs something due in change from the note I had left for him, but he was adamant about handing it over. I waved it away and shook my head, meaning to convey that he had come to the wrong party, or was welcome to keep the change and shut up, whichever interpretation he favoured; but he was not having it. He laboriously totted up the price of two coffees, plus fifteen per cent service charge, in words of one syllable, until he was satisfied that he had got it through my head. He got it right through Mr Baker's head, too. There was an audible slam as he clamped his lips together and another as he shot back his chair. Then he glared at us both with deepest loathing and stalked away.

(v)

Naturally, we wrangled about it all the way home, Robin insisting that if I had obeyed orders the débâcle would have been avoided, and my pointing out that only my intervention had saved him from getting the brush-off in the first thirty seconds.

'And you realise what that means?' I said. 'If we hadn't needled him to the point where he practically lost control, we should never have caught him out in that whopping lie.'

'And he would never have caught you out in a whopping lie, either. I should say the honours were about even.'

'But listen, why do you suppose he was at such pains to convince us that he and Adela were not speaking? Since he knew about that telephone call to Jonathan's father, he must have talked to her as recently as last night, or this morning.'

'I don't know. One would have thought it quite natural for them to hang together in a crisis like this, but of course people might not feel that, if they had something to hide. They might feel that the moment had come to draw back.'

'Do you suppose they hatched a plot to dispose of his wife and at the same time incriminate her husband? That would be a neat scheme.'

'But not a feasible one. Their alibis have been checked and re-checked, and even you and I know that he had witnesses to testify for him during the whole period.'

'Yes, but they're a cunning pair, I dare say. He strikes me as a bit of a weakling, but I'm sure Adela's the ruthless type, and clever with it. I do think we ought to go and buy that poodle, after all.'

'Too late now; the shops will be shut. You can see to it on Monday, but there's something I want you to do first; as soon as we get home, in fact.'

'What is it?'

'Ring up Mrs Müller and thank her for recommending the hairdresser. Say you've been along there and are very pleased and so on.'

'All right, but what sort of a trick is that?'

'No trick; on the contrary. The fact is that Baker has now tumbled to the fact that our running into him was no accident. There's nothing to be done about that, but with any luck he'll write it off as vulgar British curiosity. On the other hand, we may as well keep it as an isolated incident. The last thing we want is to put them on their guard.'

'What's all this got to do with the hairdresser?'

'Well, don't you see, if Mrs Müller learns that you've visited Mireille, and maybe even that you were asking rather a lot of questions, it's conceivable that she and Baker would compare notes and come up with the same answer. If you are quite open about it, the chances are that she'll take it at face value and not give it another thought.'

'Very sound reasoning,' I replied. 'Let's hope she falls for it.'

'Oh, she will,' he told me cheerfully. 'You're not half the actress I've always thought you, if you can't put across a little deception like that.'

It was not deficiencies in that line, however, which let me down, but the absence of anyone to play the scene with.

Ellen had arrived home ahead of us and was sitting with her feet propped on another chair, reading 'The Waiting Room'.

'The patient may never walk again,' she informed us, 'and I fell over twice. It was vachement humiliating.'

'Neither of us will leave Paris with a single limb intact, at this rate,' I said. 'What do you think of the script?'

'Not bad. Super, in fact.'

'You astound me. I wasn't all that taken with it.'

'Did you finish it?'

'Not yet. About halfway through.'

'You should have another go. It's the second half which is the spell-binder.'

'Well, well! You and my agent are of the same mind, it seems.'

'Your agent?' she asked blankly. 'What's she got to do with it?'

'Far be it from me to put a spoke in your career,' Robin interrupted plaintively, 'but weren't you going to make a telephone call?'

'Far be it from me to put a spoke in your career, either,' I said, emerging from my bedroom a few minutes later, 'but there was no reply to my telephone call.'

'Who were you trying to get?' Ellen asked.

'Only Mrs Müller. I thought it would be civil to thank her for giving me the name of her hairdresser. They've done quite a good job, don't you think?'

'Not bad. I'm not bowled over.'

'Nor am I, and there's absolutely no urgency about it. I can try again later.'

'You won't be able to reach her before tomorrow night, though.'

'Oh? How do you know?'

'They've bought some old barn near Caen, they're converting. They spend every Saturday and Sunday there. Jono told me. He says it's going to be very "luxe".'

'Oh well, no matter; I can do it on Monday. The hair-dressers are closed on Monday,' I explained to Robin in a meaning aside.

'All the same, it might be an idea to write her a note,' he said. 'Otherwise it'll get forgotten, for sure. I presume letters are delivered on Mondays?'

'Yes, they are, but how am I expected to write them with this blessed hand?'

'You'll manage. It only needs a couple of lines.'

'Do as he says,' Ellen told me. 'And I'll post it for you this evening.'

'Oh, don't bother. He's making a lot of heavy weather over it, but there's no hurry. Tomorrow will do quite well.'

'I'm going out, anyway.'

'Where to?' I asked sharply.

'Some friends of Jono's. He's calling for me at seven.'

'Who are they?'

'Don't worry, I've written down their name and address. It's Avenue President Wilson. You couldn't get much stuffier than that, could you?'

'Maybe not, but what are you going to do there?'

'Nothing. Play a few records, I suppose. Anyway, they're French, so their parents are sure to be barging in and out. You're always telling me I don't make enough of my opportunities to learn French, so you ought to be pleased.'

'It seems a long way to go, just to do nothing and play records,' I said snappishly, and she gaped at me in blank amazement.

'Do you approve of this?' I asked, when Ellen had gone to change and I had laboured my way through a note to Thea Müller.

'Of what?' Robin asked.

'Ellen getting so mixed up with this Jonathan.'

'Why not? It sounds quite harmless, and pretty much the kind of thing she would be doing with some boy in London; traipsing around to other people's houses to listen to records.'

'With the difference that she doesn't know any boys in London whose stepfathers have been arrested and whose mothers are having affairs with dubious Australians.'

'That's not the boy's fault, and anyway what do you expect me to do about it?'

'I don't know. Resolve the conflict for me, I suppose. Instinct says I ought to stamp on her going out with anyone connected with the Carlsens, but it seems mean to cut her off from the one friend she has made. It must be terribly dull for her with only Lupe for company, when I'm working all day. I was hoping she might enrol for French classes and meet people that way, but she seems to have gone off the idea now that Jonathan's turned up. Oh, what an evil day it was when that flight of ours was delayed! If it hadn't been for that we should never have met these people.'

'I wouldn't be too sure. I have the feeling there's a guiding hand somewhere behind it all.'

'You don't think I ought to send a cable to Toby?'

'Certainly not. It would only be an attempt to shift the responsibility and Toby's the expert at that game. He could beat you hands down any day of the week. Besides, you wouldn't have much hope of getting an answer before Ellen goes out this evening.'

'That's true. So what do you advise?'

'Why not have a talk with the little lad, yourself? He'll be here quite soon and you can draw him out a bit, in your subtle fashion, and find out what sort of a creature there is under all the sulks and self-pity. Your insight isn't too bad, as a rule.'

'All right, I will. When the bell rings, grab Ellen and keep her away from the hall. Pretend you want some help with the drinks, or any old excuse that occurs to you. I only need about five minutes.'

He agreed to co-operate and at the first trill of the bell I plunged into the hall, while he sped off to form himself into a barricade between me and Ellen's room. It was a well co-ordinated operation, with only one trifling hitch to mar its perfection. When I posted myself at the Judas hole, it was not Jonathan I saw on the landing, but Mademoiselle Pêche.

I wasted no time in studying her behaviour patterns, for it would have been obvious to a meaner intelligence that she was in a state of extreme agitation. She was dabbing at her nose and mouth with a lace handkerchief and I felt ashamed of taking even momentary advantage of her. I pulled the door open, flicked on an expression of mild surprise and bade her enter.

'Forgive my troubling you, madame, but could I have a few words in private?'

'Yes, certainly. We'll go in my bedroom. My husband and cousin are here, but they won't disturb us. May I offer you a drink?' I asked, leading the way.

Robin and Ellen had both adjourned to the kitchen and I could hear their voices over the sound of running taps.

'Just some mineral water, if it would not be troubling you too much, madame,' Mademoiselle Pêche replied, removing her black kid gloves and permitting herself one swift, appraising glance round the bedroom.

'Yes, of course. Do sit down and I'll go and get it.'

'That didn't take long,' Robin said, glancing up as I entered the kitchen.

'One scotch and soda, please,' I said, 'and one Vichy for the visitor. The visitor is Miss Pêche and she has private matters to impart. So you will have to manage without me for the time being,' I added, fixing him with a look which was meant to speak volumes.

I returned to Miss Pêche, who was sitting bolt upright on a bedroom chair, with her ankles crossed. Her shoes were trim and stubby and looked as though they might have been bought in Oxford Street twenty years ago.

'You have a very good apartment, madame,' she informed me grandly.

'Oh yes. Thank you. It's not bad. The furniture doesn't belong to us, of course.'

'No, that is to be expected. It would not be practical for such a short stay,' she replied, explaining the obvious.

I was still hoping to conclude the interview before Jonathan came and went and I said:

'Is there something I can do for you? Or for Mr Carlsen?'

'I have been to see him,' she answered in less stilted tones, relieved perhaps to have the civilities chopped off.

'How is he?'

'He is well. He does not complain. The food is not bad,' she added, as an afterthought.

'And so he is allowed to have visitors?'

'One every day, apart from his lawyer. I, myself, go every day.'

'How about his wife?'

'He has asked her not to come. He says she can only distress herself. Ah, madame, if you could only know the goodness of that man, there is nothing . . . Never to complain of his situation! Always thinking of others and sparing them, if he can.'

It occurred to me that, if the police were correct in their assumptions, he had not been over-vigilant in sparing Mrs Baker, but I refrained from striking this discordant note. Anyone could see that in the eyes of the devoted Pêche, Sven was a martyr and a hero, and the possibility of his guilt had never entered her head. I said:

'So what is there I can do?'

'Madame, I have a favour to beg of you. I am hoping you can accommodate me.'

'I'll try.'

'Mr Carlsen is allowed to read, but he does not find much to interest him in . . . where he is, and he likes most of all to read English works.'

'You mean that you wish to borrow some? Well, you are welcome to anything we have, but I'm afraid they aren't very thick on the ground. Just two or three novels and some magazines we bought for the journey, and that's about all. I'll go and see what I can dig up for you.'

'Thank you, madame, you are very kind. Anything at all, you understand, so long as it is in English.'

There was still no sign of Jonathan, but Robin and Ellen had moved into the salon. I got them both on their feet to join in the literature hunt, but it did not yield much of a harvest and only took us a few minutes. In that time we managed to dredge up four magazines, two paperback crime stories and a volume of plays by Chekov. I rejected Ellen's copy of *The Naked Lunch*, on the grounds that Miss Pêche might read it first and form a low opinion of our moral standards.

As it happened, I formed rather a low opinion of her moral standards when I returned from this fray. My bedroom door was shut, and being one-handed I was obliged to place my trophies on the floor in order to open it. Before bending down again, I caught a glimpse of her back, leaning over the writing-desk. There was a click as of a drawer being shut, but when I entered the room she had straightened up and turned to face me. So far as I could see, nothing on my desk had been disturbed and the letter to Mrs Müller was lying where I had left it.

'Not a very exciting collection, I'm afraid,' I said, proffering my pile, and could tell from her expression that she agreed with me.

'If you could give me some idea of the kind of thing he enjoys, I'll go to a bookshop and see what I can find.'

'That is not at all what I am asking, madame.'

'Why not? Don't worry about the expense or anything. We should be glad to help, in whatever way we can.'

'But, I assure you, it is not gifts he is seeking. This he would not accept, madame. It is simply the loan of something to read, which would be returned to you in only a few days.'

'Then I am sorry, but this is the best we can do. Has he no other English-speaking friends you could ask?'

'Yes, without doubt, but Mr Carlsen wishes me to approach you, before anyone. To be frank, madame, there is a unique way you could be of assistance to him.'

'Then please tell me what it is.'

'I must explain that, as well as reading, he is hoping to pass some of this difficult time by writing some things of his own.'

'That sounds sensible, but how on earth could we help there? You mean, he needs a typewriter, or paper? If so . . .'

'No, no, not that, but you understand, do you not, that he is deeply interested in matters of the cinema and theatre?'

'No,' I said slowly, 'I can't say I had understood that. Now you mention it.'

'It is true, however. Perhaps he was too shy to tell you, but he admires you extremely, as an artist, and I think this is why he turns to you now. He is anxious to try his hand at writing a scenario, but he does not know all about the technical side. It occurs to him that you might have some material of that kind which he could study.'

'You mean other people's scripts?'

'Please, madame, if you have any and would be so kind as to spare them. It would mean so much, and they would all be returned to you; you have my word for it.'

The doorbell rang as she spoke, and it recalled to me the first occasion when I had heard it, sitting in the bath exactly a week ago. It had signified the mysterious return of my red suitcase and it flashed into my mind that all the play-acting and subterfuge denoted not that something had been removed from its contents, but that something had been added to them.

'Excuse me,' I said, getting up. 'A friend has arrived and I have to see him for a moment. I shan't be long.'

This time I drew the door to as I went out, but left it unlatched. I could hear voices from the salon, Robin's predominating, and silently applauded him for taking over the interrogation. Then I darted across to Ellen's room and shut myself in. The pages of 'The Waiting Room' were scattered about on her bed. I tucked them neatly back into their folder and, for good measure, pushed it under the eiderdown. Then I stood at the window for a bit, doing breathing exercises.

Mademoiselle Pêche was sitting demurely where I had left her and since I knew she had not found what she had come for, I concluded that she was confident of having bamboozled me into handing it over voluntarily. A disappointment was in store:

'Sorry about that,' I said, 'but while I was out there I asked my husband's advice. You see, it so happens that I do have one or two scripts with me, but they're only on loan. My husband agrees that I am not entitled to let them out of my hands, even in a special case like this.'

'It would only be for one or two days, madame. I would return them to you personally, on Monday or Tuesday. You have my word.'

'I'm not doubting it for an instant,' I lied, 'but I'm afraid I must stick to what my husband says. He's a police detective, as you've probably heard, so he knows the form about these things. You see, there are very strict copyright laws. I'll show you.'

I hauled the red case down from my wardrobe and flicked open the lid. The two folders from my agent's office were lying on top, and choosing the one called 'Thursday Never Comes', I held it out to her. She barely gave it a glance.

'But, madame, I am not ignorant of these things. I, too, have many confidential documents in my care. But have you no others, not so private? Some old material, which is now out of date?'

'No, I haven't. It's not the kind of thing one carts around when travelling abroad. It's possible that I could get hold of some for you. It may take a little time, but if you wish I'll see what I can do.'

'Please don't trouble yourself, madame. There has been some misunderstanding. Mr Carlsen was certain . . .'

'Of what?'

She regarded me squarely: 'That you would be able to help him.'

'That's too bad, and I'm sorry that I cannot.'

I stood up, meaning to terminate the interview, but Ellen forestalled me. She banged on the door and stuck her head round, saying:

'The inquisition's over and we're just off. Robin asked me to come and get your letter.'

'Here it is, and don't go stashing it away in that great rucksack of yours and then forget all about it.'

'No, I won't,' she replied amiably, 'since it does seem to be rather urgent, after all.'

'Would you mind awfully if we stayed in tonight?' I asked Robin, as soon as we were alone. I had temporarily lost interest in the problem of Jonathan and had only paid token attention to the assurances that he seemed to be a nice enough boy, underneath all the fringes and glooms.

'Not at all. Any particular reason? Your hand's not hurting, is it?'

'Not any more. I think I'll take this bandage off tomorrow. No, the fact is there's a script I ought to read.'

'Really? Any hurry about it?'

'I believe so,' I admitted. 'I really believe the time has come to find out what Ellen noticed and I missed.'

(vi)

'Of course, I'd have spotted it myself,' I explained, one hour later. 'Ellen was quite right; the most interesting part comes in the second half. Where is Ellen, by the way? It must be getting awfully late.'

'Only half past nine, so don't start sending cables yet,' Robin answered, breaking off his own study of the script. He had started from scratch the minute I put it down and was three quarters of the way through.

'Well, do hurry up with that. I'm dying to hear your views.'

'Patience, please! I need ten more minutes, which will only turn into twenty if you don't stop prattling.'

Twenty minutes later to the dot, he replaced the last sheet in the folder and laid it on the table between us.

'Now be an angel and make some fresh coffee, while I collect my wits.'

'Oh, honestly, Robin, how maddening you can be sometimes!'

'And make it a little stronger this time,' he added, as I did a bit of flouncing out.

'When you talk of the most interesting part,' he said, as I returned with the steaming pot, 'I suppose you refer to the girl's murder?'

'Well, naturally.'

The coffee was the colour and consistency of tar. He took one sip and for a moment we both thought he was going to spit it out. Restraining himself, he went on:

'We are also assuming that this story, "The Waiting Room", was written by Carlsen, alias Henry Fitzgerald?'

'Yes, we are. It explains so many puzzles.'

'Though not, by any means, all. In fact, I should say it creates as many puzzles as it solves. Why, for instance, was

he so keen to plant it on you, only to go to equally complicated lengths to get it back again?'

'We only have Pêche's word for it that he is trying to get
it back again, and she could be acting for someone else. She
pretends to be deeply concerned about Sven, but it might be
just an act. After all, he didn't give her a note for me, which
would have been the normal thing. In fact, you know, Robin,
it struck me even at the time that she was inventing that bit
about his wanting scripts for models. Otherwise, why not
have said so from the start? I think she was hoping to get
her hands on it either by pinching it while I was out of the
room, or by trickery. When both those failed, she launched
into this other tale. But if he is the author of "The Waiting
Room", which we both agree he must be, he wouldn't need
models at this stage. He knows enough about the technical-
ities already to turn out a rough scenario and the shooting
script would come much later.'

'All right; but assuming that he did write it and that he
did put it in your suitcase, why all the subterfuge?'

'But that's so typical of him. He's conceited, in a rather
childish way, and I'm sure he thought I had only to read it
to be dazzled by its brilliance. But he probably also guessed
that lots of people send me scripts to read and most of them
just lie around for ages. Whereas, if I believed it had come
to me through my agent, I'd be much more likely to give it
serious attention.'

'His methods were rather drastic, weren't they?'

'Yes, but with just the kind of cloak-and-dagger element
that would appeal to him. You can tell from the script just
what kind of schoolboy fantasy world he lives in.'

'So the next thing one asks oneself is: which came first,
the chicken or the egg?'

'That is the kind of question which people always ask themselves out loud and I never know what they mean.'

'In this case, it means: did the fiction or the fact come first? In all the essentials, the real-life murder was identical to the one he describes in the script.'

The episode to which he referred came towards the end of 'The Waiting Room' and it was true that the similarities between it and Leila Baker's death were quite remarkable. In the script the victim was a patient, a psychopathic, adolescent girl, with strong tendencies to nymphomania, kleptomania and spiteful curiosity, among other unfortunate traits. As had been inevitable from her first appearance, this unattractive character had presented a dire threat to Dr Marcus, who was the real villain of the piece, with the result that she had got her come-uppance before she had a chance to cook his goose. It was her murder that created the springboard from which Simon Charrington was able to plunge into the final derring-do sequence, killing off numerous baddies and triumphantly delivering the captive psychiatrist into the hands of the Allies. Meanwhile, Delphine, the beautiful nurse, had emerged in her true colours, and it was thanks to her selfless courage that he was able to bring off this dazzling coup. Unfortunately, she had been mortally wounded in the process and the story had faded out with her sighing and dying in his arms, like a sweet Victorian heroine. It was all fairly absurd, but the really riveting feature was that the murdered girl had first been knocked unconscious and then strangled with her own two plaits.

'There is a third possibility,' I said, 'though I have no idea where it figures in your chicken and egg syndrome.'

'Perhaps it will turn out to be the bacon?'

'Suppose there were three murders? Two in real life and the fictitious one in the middle?'

'Meaning that something like this happened a long while ago and Carlsen pinched the idea for his script? Surely we'd have heard about it?'

'Not necessarily, if it happened in a foreign country.'

'So you think this Doctor Somebody-or-Other could have been based on a real person?'

'Felix Marcus. You should remember the name because the initials are rather significant.'

'Yes, so they are!'

'And Dr Müller was in charge of a clinic in Germany, where Sven's first wife was a patient. How about that? It was a T.B. clinic, actually, but that's a detail.'

'I didn't know that.'

'He mentioned it himself, when he was driving us home, but I expect you forgot because it was immediately after that that we had the panic over the keys.'

'Which reminds me that the key business is another unsolved mystery. Did Sven take them, and, if so, was it in order to break in and retrieve his script? Then why did he plant it on you in the first place? We're back to that again.'

'He may not have stolen them. They could have dropped out of your pocket, as Pêche claimed, or she could have pinched them herself. Your macintosh was sitting in Sven's office for all of two hours and perhaps she's working for Dr Müller on the side.'

'The theory being that this psychopathic girl really existed and was murdered by Franz Müller, alias Felix Marcus?'

'Why not?'

'So, having disposed of her, he chugs merrily along on his espionage course, only to be tripped up by Mrs Baker when he arrives in Paris. Do you suppose the motive in her case was the same, or has he got a phobia about women with long hair?'

'Laugh if you like, but having got away with it once why shouldn't he have used the same method again? Specially if he believed that no living soul knew about the first time.'

'But how did he then discover that Sven did know and had written it into his script? He must have been aware of that, if he was really behind Pêche in her efforts to get it back from you.'

'Probably Pêche told him. What more natural than that she should have read the script? And if she's in league with Müller her job would be to scrape up any information she could, and pass it on. She told me herself that she handled a lot of confidential documents.'

'You could hardly describe "The Waiting Room" in those terms,' Robin objected.

'No, and I don't suppose she did, either, until Leila Baker was killed. Then the coincidence would have struck her and force of habit would have made her tell Dr Müller. It must have given him quite a frisson to learn that the very colleague he'd been double-crossing was in possession of evidence to get him convicted of murder. I bet he didn't lose any time instructing Pêche to get hold of the script and destroy it, before Sven could tell anyone where he got the idea from, and before the police started asking awkward questions.'

'They wouldn't restrict themselves to questions, you know. They'd check with the German authorities, as well.'

'Yes, but if he'd disposed of the girl's body and covered his tracks, it's unlikely that anything incriminating could be traced to him. So long as the script was destroyed and Pêche sworn to secrecy, it would be hard to prove that Sven hadn't invented the story, as a lunatic attempt to put the blame on someone else. Pêche is at great pains to create the impression that she's loyalty personified, so no one would suspect her of telling lies to get Sven into trouble.'

'And we don't know that she has told any. All she has said is that Sven was in his office at seven-twenty on the night of the murder, which does nothing either to exonerate or incriminate him.'

'But supposing it were actually fifteen or twenty minutes later than that when she went back and saw him working? That would mean that when Mrs Müller saw him leave the building, he would have been coming down from his office, just as she thought. He certainly wouldn't have had time to get to the Champ de Mars and back.'

'And neither, I must point out, would he have had time to get to the cinema.'

'Oh damn, nor he would,' I admitted sadly. 'We go round and round and we always end by running straight into the same old obstacle.'

'Well, cheer up; we may have cleared away a little of the undergrowth. I'll pay another round of courtesy calls on Monday and see if there's a dossier on Dr Müller. Their records are pretty exhaustive.'

'Records?' I repeated stupidly.

'Not Ellen's variety. Wake up, Tessa! You've gone all gormless.'

'I know it. My gorm deserted me days ago and it's only just trickling back. Of course, Dr Müller has a record. Sven told me. He's done a stretch.'

'Here, in France?'

'No, Germany.'

'What was the charge? Not homicide, by any chance?'

'Well yes, it was, that's the extraordinary thing. He was run in for knocking off one of his patients with the wrong dose. Not malice aforethought, you understand; criminal negligence.'

'But we know better?'

'Do we?' I asked in a hopeless voice. 'I'm beginning to feel that we know worse and worse. You see, it was Sven who insisted that the charge was a trumped-up one, just an excuse to lock him up. He said the real reason was that they didn't like his politics. That doesn't fit very well with Dr Felix, does it?'

Robin said thoughtfully: 'I wouldn't be too depressed by that, if I were you. He had already planted the script on you by then, but he hadn't reckoned on your meeting Dr Müller. That was an unfortunate accident, so he quickly set about impressing on you that Müller had been imprisoned for political rather than criminal activities. In that way he would hope to prevent your associating the two characters; and, indeed, I doubt very much if you ever would have, if it hadn't been for the real murder following so quickly.'

'All of which is another indication that Sven is not a likely person to have committed it.'

'And also that it wouldn't hurt to start a few enquiries about Dr Müller. Something may turn up in the records.'

'There you go again!' I moaned. 'I do wish we had a different word for it, like the French. What time is it now, and why isn't she back?'

'Only just after ten, but you could give those people a blow of the telephone and ask them to put her in a taxi. You've got their number.'

'I suppose I'll have to,' I agreed, 'even though it may be a rod in pickle. I'll feel worse than ever if they tell me she left hours ago.'

I was spared this ordeal, however, because Ellen turned up before I had finished dialling. Jonathan was with her and remained scowling in the background, while she led off with the explanations.

'His mother's gone to the country. He was invited too, but he didn't fancy it. He doesn't much fancy being alone in their flat, either, so we thought the best thing would be for him to come here. He can sleep on the floor, if it's okay with you.'

'Oh, perfectly,' I agreed. 'The only thing is, he may be rather uncomfortable. I don't think these French floors were really made for sleeping on.'

'I'll be okay,' Jonathan mumbled, in his usual ebullient fashion.

'Where's Adela gone?' I asked, as Ellen and I laid out cushions and coats on the slithery parquet.

'To the Müllers' place in Normandy. The Frau rang up at lunch-time and made a great point of it.'

'Why didn't Jonathan want to go? I thought it was so plushy there? I'm sure he'd have been much more comfortable than with this lot.'

'Part of it is, but they're only halfway through the conversions. Jonathan has to sleep in some dreary bit of the stables. It's miles away from the house, and I think he's a bit nervous, actually. Besides, there's another reason why he hates going there. That Doctor Müller is an awful drag.'

'Really? He struck me as a rather cuddlesome old party, except when he gets behind the steering-wheel.'

'That's only his act. The driving Müller is the real one. Jono says he's a fantastic sadist and bully, so he tries to keep out of his way as much as possible, and who can blame him?'

'Who, indeed?' I agreed, making a neat job of folding the sheet over my red velvet evening cloak.

Nine

AT DAYBREAK on Sunday while the juveniles slumbered on, the even tenor of our days took another beating, in the form of a telephone call from my cousin Toby. He was speaking from Cherbourg.

'What are you doing in Cherbourg?' I asked.

'A curious question! If you must know, I am making a very expensive telephone call to a half-wit in Paris.'

'I beg your pardon. I should have said: how did you get to Cherbourg?'

'On an ocean liner. I didn't get your cable, by the way.'

'I've sent so many cables. Which one didn't you get?'

'The one about my opening night. It was last Thursday. Not even a postcard.'

'If you've come all the way to Cherbourg to tell me that,' I said, 'I have news for you.'

'Well, I haven't. I had this insane idea that it might be better to travel on a French liner, instead of that rolling Odeon they carried me out on.'

'Was it?'

'Very slightly. Hardly worth the bother, though, when you consider where it has landed me.'

I asked him how the first night had gone and, between all the grousings, there were hints that he was not wholly displeased. Apparently, the play had got a rapturous reception and advance bookings were rocketing. All of which, he explained, was further proof of the total lack of discrimination of American audiences, since, conceivably, no worse acted or directed piece had reached the stage within living memory.

'How's Ellen?' he then enquired.

'Fine, just fine. I'd put her on the line, only she's not awake yet.'

'I was wondering if I was going to see you?'

'Ob, certainly, if you feel like coming into Paris. I'm afraid we can't offer you a bed and the floor space is a little crowded at present, but . . .'

'Oh, I wasn't thinking of that,' he assured me hastily. 'I hate Paris and I'm catching a boat home tomorrow. There seems to be some kind of ferry service. I thought you might all drive up here for lunch.'

'Well, I don't know,' I said doubtfully. 'My geography is not very hot, but it's a hell of a way, isn't it?'

'Haven't you got a car?'

I explained that the studios had provided me with one for the travelling to work and that I had a separate arrangement with the driver for using it privately, adding:

'But this is Sunday.'

'I know that; it is here, too.'

'I mean, he may not be available. He's probably taking the wife and little ones to la plage and la mer.'

'There's plenty of mer here. Rather too much, as it happens. But still, I see what you mean. Why not ask him? Failing that, there must be other ways of hiring a car in Paris?'

'I'll go into conference with Robin,' I said, 'and ring you back.'

More than an hour had passed before I was able to do so, mainly owing to that particular brand of inertia and procrastination which is liable to overtake any group of people, when required to make decisions on Sunday morning.

Robin was unenthusiastic about the project, which he rightly envisaged as both expensive and exhausting, but was nevertheless prepared to sink his own wishes in favour of the majority. Ellen was eager to go, but dubious about leaving Jonathan on his own. After much entreaty, Jonathan ungraciously consented to accompany us, but just when all seemed in a fair way to being settled, abruptly changed his mind and said that he preferred to stay at home. I had a sinking feeling that by 'home' he now meant 108 Avenue de Suffren and redoubled my efforts to herd the entire flock into one pen.

The only tall, straight reed among us was Pierre, who had responded to my enquiries by presenting himself and his Citroen within twenty minutes of the summons. Having been sized up through the spy-hole and admitted by Ellen, he was obliged to spend the ensuing half hour sitting around and drinking coffee, while the rest of us drooped about, arguing the toss and letting the precious minutes slip through our nerveless fingers. It was he who finally brought order to this chaos by coming up with the compromise so dear to the hearts of all true vacillators.

His simple suggestion, delivered in the form of a lengthy and rather impassioned monologue, was that instead of driving all the way to Cherbourg, we should meet Toby somewhere along the route. Lisieux was the place he recommended, where there was a Gothic cathedral meriting a glance. In this way, Pierre reminded us, we should halve our travelling time and enable ourselves to take the little promenade and the little apéritifs, so essential for working up an appetite for lunch.

Even Jonathan regarded this proposal favourably, although he found it necessary to go to the bathroom and brood for twenty minutes before giving it the seal of his approval.

Pierre had patently considered luncheon to be the cornerstone of the excursion and when I re-established contact with Cherbourg I found that Toby's mind ran on the same lines. The only stipulation was that we should not eat it in

Lisieux, which would be crammed to suffocation with Gothic-cathedral fans. His Michelin guide revealed that, twenty kilometres to the east, at a village called Assy-les-Cygnes, was to be found the Auberge du Père Bernard, whose entry was embellished with an impressive number of stars, knives and forks and songbirds.

It only remained for Robin to calculate how his store of travellers' cheques would stand up to such onslaughts, Jonathan to emerge from the bathroom and Ellen to set her tartan cap at the right angle, for the whole party to be on its way.

We reached Lisieux soon after midday and tracked Toby down behind a copy of *France-Dimanche* outside a café in the main square and catching up, as he explained, with the domestic life of the Royal family. He was full of grumbles about the heat and boredom of his journey, but I could tell that he was really in good spirits and that the play's success still fired an inner glow.

Ellen must have sensed it, too, for after our little promenade she readily agreed to drive with him to the next stop, despite repeated advance warnings that she was not to be left alone with him for a single second, lest the dreaded Margaret Hacker should rear her head.

They set out ahead of us, Toby's driver claiming to know the way, and leaving Jonathan to travel with Robin and me. We put him in front beside Pierre, whose overtures he ignored, preferring to stare stonily out of the side window.

'Your little old cousin is in great form,' Robin remarked.

'Yes, isn't he? If Ellen plays it diplomatically, I doubt if Margaret will even get a mention. Let's just pray this restaurant turns out to be as rare and beautiful as he . . .'

'Where's this guy supposed to be taking us?' Jonathan interrupted, turning round with an enraged look on his face.

'To Assy-les-Cygnes, don't you remember? Oh no, he wasn't there when it was all decided, was he, Robin? It's where we're going to have lunch.'

'Why there, for Chrissake?'

'Because Ellen's father knows a good place. Any objection?'

Obviously, he had plenty, but we did not hear about them because we were entering the outskirts of the little town and, on rounding a bend into the main street, Pierre had been obliged, with many a Gallic oath, to stand on the brake in order to avoid colliding with the back of Toby's car.

The street was just wide enough to allow for the passage of two vehicles, but not even the passage of one was being allowed at this time, nor had been, I judged, for some time past. We were situated at the crest of a gentle slope which descended in a straight line for about a quarter of a mile, and then rose again for the same distance on the other side. Thus, we had a comprehensive view of the half mile of road ahead of us, which was stacked from end to end with stationary traffic. Only the actual cause of the blockage was concealed from us and must have been at the lowest point between the two hills.

Being temperamentally unsuited to waiting for things to get better or worse, some of the drivers were playing tunes on their horns, while others had lazily pressed their thumbs down and left them to sound a continuous blare. Several had emerged from their cars and were running about and taking the opportunity to make long speeches at each other.

Both Pierre and Toby's driver belonged to this category and, after a short but heated argument on the pavement, set off down the hill towards the heart of the fraças.

Long acquaintance with Toby's claustrophobia and aversion to noise warned me that it would need more than diplomacy on Ellen's part to avert a crisis if this situation were to be prolonged, and said peevishly:

'I do wish Pierre wasn't so impetuous. If only he had kept his head and backed out we might have found another route round.'

'Well, it's too late to think of that now,' Robin informed me, craning his head to see through the rear window. 'There are at least half a dozen more behind us and the front one is stepping on our tail.'

'Let's get out and stroll a bit ourselves, then. I've got the cooped-up feeling.'

Toby had it, too. He and Ellen had decided to proceed to the restaurant on foot, their driver having assured them it was not far, and downhill all the way. Greatly as he detested exercise of any kind, Toby was prepared to consider any means of escape from the existing torture.

'Come on!' I said. 'Let's all go. We have nothing to lose but our way.'

'We can't very well abandon the cars completely,' Robin pointed out. 'There could be a move at any minute.'

'I don't mind staying till those guys get back,' Jonathan said, showing hitherto unrevealed traces of humanity.

'How very sweet of you!' I exclaimed effusively, paying the exaggerated tribute which is so often bestowed on disagreeable people when they display a modicum of decency.

'But he can't drive both cars,' Robin objected.

'I'll manage okay. They won't move too fast to start with, and if I have to I'll just let go the handbrake so they slide down.'

'I'll stay, too,' Ellen said, causing Toby to lose his frail, finger-tip hold on patience:

'Oh, stop being boy scouts, both of you. There isn't a sign of movement anywhere. Even when they've tidied up whatever it is, it will be hours before anything moves up here, and personally I don't care what they do.'

Saying this, he turned away and stumped off down the pavement. Ellen looked uncertainly at each of us, then skidded away and caught up with Toby. Jonathan leant back in his seat and folded his arms:

'I'm staying right where I am,' he announced mulishly.

'Please yourself,' Robin told him. 'I don't imagine Pierre will be long. If you're still stuck when he gets back I suggest you get the other driver to direct you to the restaurant. You remember what it's called?'

'Sure!'

'And you'd better ask them to bring both cars there at three, to pick us up.'

'Kay.'

'What a strange boy!' I remarked, as we ambled down the hill.

'Ghastly. Not altogether his fault, perhaps. He comes from a strange family.'

It was not until we were nearly at the bottom that we found the obstruction which was causing all the trouble. The village at this point was divided through the middle by a shallow, high-banked stream and the ancient bridge which spanned it was just wide enough for a single vehicle. Poised on top of this bridge, and leading the oncoming traffic, was a shabby little country bus. There was space for the driver to proceed in safety and the traffic going in our direction had halted far enough back for him to do so. The snag was that on the right-hand side of the road, on the corner of a lane which ran alongside the stream, a vast Buick with a green number-plate had been parked half in the road and half on the pavement, but with its front wheels and bonnet jutting over the lane. This was at the very point where the main road narrowed down to the width of the bridge. A small crowd had collected to watch the fun, and a sergent de ville was straddled across his motor-bike, communing with his walkie-talkie, but no one seemed willing to take any practical steps to alleviate the situation.

'One of your spies, no doubt,' I remarked to Robin, as, still following the other two, we edged round the front of the car and into the lane.

'Not a very efficient one,' he replied. 'One could hardly applaud him for drawing attention to himself quite so blatantly.'

'Ah, that's probably just his cunning. He is creating a diversion, so that he can do the real spying somewhere else.'

'You have an answer for everything,' Robin said, but it did not escape me that he made a note of the licence number.

The Auberge du Père Bernard was a mere five minutes' walk from the bridge, a cosy, farmhouse kind of building, with a garden bordering the banks of the stream, and a sight to restore our jaded spirits. Toby had booked a table and we were royally received, despite being ten minutes late for our appointment.

'For five, isn't it?' the patron asked, looking faintly mystified.

'For five,' Toby agreed. 'There is one more to come. We shall consult the menu while we wait for him.'

It was the size of a pillowcase, written in dashing violet ink and more like a gastronomic adventure-story than a menu. When we had studied, argued, studied again and changed our minds half a dozen times, Jonathan had still not arrived.

'I don't think we need wait any longer before ordering, do we?' Toby asked. 'Or do we?'

Ellen, who had been the principal target for these questions, was studying an illustrated map of the region on the back of the menu card.

'No need at all,' she answered. 'He'll only want biftek and frites, when he does come.'

There was only one major topic of conversation during the ensuing twenty minutes, which was a fair compliment to the Pere's cuisine, and I drew Toby's attention to the fact that people are more inclined to discuss food and wine when they are enjoying it than at any other time.

'Which is why the French talk about it more often than we do,' he replied. 'In England it is considered poor taste to talk about what one is eating, and in most houses it would be. If only Ellen had plodded on with Megs Witherspoon, ours might have been one of the laudable exceptions. But, heigh-ho, it was not to be.'

'You'd have hated it,' Ellen told him crossly. 'The only thing we learnt was how to cut up tomatoes to make them look like roses.'

'Oh well,' he admitted. 'I do prefer my roses to be made of rose, it's true; but I daresay you would have graduated to something more practical as time went on.'

It was plain that he was faintly put out by having his little pleasantry so severely stamped on, and it was so far outside Ellen's nature to be snappy that I guessed that Jonathan's continued absence must be to blame. I leant across the table, saying in a low voice:

'Cheer up! I'm sure he'll be here soon.'

'I'm sure he won't,' she retorted crisply.

As a matter of fact, I was inclined to agree with her, but we were unable to prolong this unprofitable exchange because a waiter had materialised and was hovering by our table. He announced to no one in particular that Mademoiselle Crichton was wanted on the telephone.

'Oh Lord!' I said, bounding to my feet. 'It must be Pierre. He's the only one who calls me that. What now, I wonder?'

The telephone was in a tiny alcove just behind the bar and there was a good deal of clatter and chatter going on around me, making it difficult to hear. A female voice, which I dimly recognised, commanded me not to quit the apparatus and was replaced by a more familiar one saying:

'Is that you, Ellie? Listen, I'm here at—'

It was just about the longest sentence I had ever heard him speak, and instead of allowing him to complete it, like any sensible person, I instinctively cut him short.

'Just a minute, Jonathan. This is Tessa speaking. Is it Ellen you want, or will I do?'

There was a brief silence and when he spoke again it was in his normal gruff and toneless manner:

'Just say I won't be along.'

'Oh, why not? Where are you speaking from?'

'Lisieux. I'm at the railroad station. I'll get a train back in.'

'Whatever for? And how did you get there? Did Pierre drive you?'

'No, there was this bus coming up. It was heading for Lisieux, so I got on.'

'But why, Jonathan? Is anything wrong?'

'Nope.'

'Are you sure?'

'Just give Ellie the message, will you?' he said and rang off.

'Any idea what it's all about?' I asked her. 'I mean, I'm all for people doing their own thing, etcetera, but this does seem to be going a bit far, in every sense. What do you make of it?'

'How would I know?' she asked indifferently.

'But I think perhaps you do,' I said, spacing the words to give them emphasis, narrowing my eyes and putting everything I'd got into the penetrating look.

It didn't even get through her outer casing. She can be very cool when she chooses and it occurred to me that, should she fail to get her foot in the theatre, she would have no trouble making a fortune at poker.

TEN

(i)

I BELIEVE the question of Ellen's returning to England with Toby was mooted and quickly dismissed. I no longer remember what excuse she made for refusing, for I had other things on my mind and had become for the time being partially oblivious to what was going on around me. However, it may well have been her reluctance which put him in such a nasty temper and ended our fête champêtre on a somewhat sour note. I do recall that, as we were leaving the restaurant and I picked up a menu card saying I would keep it as a souvenir, he asked me in waspish tones whether I did not wish to have it autographed by all present as well.

The cars arrived punctually at three, the village, now clear of obstruction and traffic, was shuttered and somnolent and we reached Lisieux in under half an hour. Here we parted company, getting a languid wave from Toby as he turned north towards Cherbourg.

Two preoccupations engrossed me at this time and since both fought equally hard for attention I found my mind switching from one to the other, without advancing a centimetre in either direction. The only hope of achieving some progress lay in an hour or two of solitude and I therefore told Robin I would forgo the pleasure of accompanying him to the airport on Monday morning. I explained that I needed time to prepare myself for work on Tuesday, for I had been able to give so little of it to the proper study of my part that, if the drift continued, I was in real danger of winning a special award at Cannes for the dullest perform-ance of the year.

His plane was scheduled to take off at two o'clock, so he had planned to have an early lunch at the airport. Pierre was to pick him up at eleven-thirty and Ellen to deputise for me in seeing him off.

Long before this, however, he had wended the now famil-iar way down to the piscine, for yet another conference with his friends in the deep end.

'You may be relieved to hear,' he told me afterwards, 'that the case is by no means closed. The Müllers and everyone else remotely connected with Mrs Baker are still being prod-ded and will be called in for more questioning whenever fresh evidence comes to light. In fact, I get the impression that everyone is prepared for the ramifications to drag on for months, or years if need be.'

'So they are not sure that Sven is guilty?'

'Well, technically he is because with the case they have built up, it is up to him to prove his innocence, not the other way round. That's the way they do things over here, but of course it doesn't always stop there.'

'And has any fresh evidence come to light?'

'In a sense, it has. The full dossier on the arrest and trial of Dr Müller has now come in from Germany. It contains some rather sensational disclosures.'

'Oh, splendid!'

'Not quite your brand of sensationalism, I must warn you. The fact is that apart from their both being doctors there is not a single point of resemblance between the careers of Dr Felix Marcus and Franz Müller.'

'You are quite right not to call it my brand,' I assured him.

'Here is something you may like better: there is very little resemblance between the true case-history of Dr Müller and the one described to you by Sven.'

'Yes, I do like that a little better, but it doesn't get us very far.'

'It tells us something rather significant about Carlsen, don't you think?'

'Like?'

'That he deluded himself as much as anyone. Would you care to hear the true facts about Müller?'

'I can't wait.'

'Well, to start with, he ran a T.B. clinic, as you already know. No suggestion of head-shrinking or of the patients being there under duress. In fact, they paid exorbitant fees for the privilege.'

'But a private hospital, and he was in sole charge?'

'Yes, but he was a highly qualified practitioner and specialist in pulmonary diseases. He'd previously worked in state hospitals, but he'd developed some very unconventional theories about the treatment for these complaints, and there lies the crux of the story.'

'Why?'

'When he found these theories weren't being taken seriously by the medical profession, he became obsessed with the dream of trying them out on his own. Hence the clinic, and hence, finally, his downfall. There is some uncertainty about how he raised the money to start it. Probably he sank all his own private means because, despite the huge fees, he was unable to pay for his defence at the trial. It was a very posh set-up, I might add, and the nurses were chosen for their looks, as well as their skill. The surroundings-beautiful was one of several crackpot ideas of therapy for these cases.'

'Why crackpot? I should think there might be a lot in it.'

'Medically speaking, it apparently doesn't matter a damn whether the patient has Helen of Troy or King Kong handing out the pills, so long as they're the right pills.'

'And were they?'

'Yes, on the whole. I gather that most of the patients who recovered would have done so anyway, under conventional treatment; and most of those who died would also have done so anyway, in the normal course of things; but there were exceptions. He did bring off one or two rather sensational cures, in cases which had been written off as hopeless. He got a good deal of publicity for these, which, as you can imagine, didn't make him any more popular with the orthodox members of his profession.'

'Who were gunning for him, I suppose?'

'Giving him enough rope to hang himself would be nearer the mark.'

'Except that he wasn't hanged. According to Sven he got four years for manslaughter. Was that true?'

'Yes, but this is where the script and the facts really do part company. There never was any young female strangled with her own hair. The case concerned a young man and he died in his bed, between midnight and three a.m. The trouble was that until then he was considered to have made such a miraculous recovery that he was due to be discharged the following week. So naturally his family raised hell, and egged on, no doubt, by other interested parties, demanded a full-scale investigation.'

'And what did that produce?'

'That he died from an overdose of an extremely dangerous drug.'

I thought this over and then said: 'It could have been suicide?'

'Suicide, accident; it makes no difference which. The point is that it amounted to criminal carelessness that such a large dose of that particular drug should have got into the wrong hands, whether the hands belonged to a patient, or to some incompetent member of the staff.'

'No question of Dr Müller being personally responsible?'

'None whatever, because no motive. It's true that he was on the premises at the time, but this young man was his star patient, a terminal case who had fully recovered. He was the last person Müller would have wished to dispose of.'

'Nevertheless, he got all the blame for it?'

'It was his own choice,' Robin explained. 'He was the sole authority for the treatment each patient received and when it came to the crunch he took sole responsibility. In any case, he probably had no option. You could say that he was morally to blame, whoever actually administered the dose.'

'And they never found out who that was?'

'The question hardly came up. There wasn't a shred of evidence to show that anyone had acted maliciously and if Müller had any ideas about it he never voiced them. As I say, he assumed full responsibility, right from the beginning.'

'But, you know, Robin, that could have been quite a shrewd move on his part. Supposing he had done it deliberately, for some motive which never came out? Then, when the investigation got going, it wouldn't have needed very quick thinking to realise that by taking that holy attitude he would be laying himself open to a few years for manslaughter, rather than a life sentence for murder.'

'When you speak of motives not coming to light, I presume you are harking back to the spy element and Dr Felix Marcus, but I assure you there's no foundation for it. Müller dedicated his whole life to that clinic. He visited each of his patients twice every day and he ate and slept on the premises. And the suggestion of his being some kind of political hothead is equally wide of the mark. Like so many of his breed, he remained outside politics all his life. You could say that he got a harsher sentence than he strictly deserved, but you don't have to invent high-flown romantic reasons for that. The hostility he had aroused and which contributed to his punishment had nothing to do with revolutionary views or communist plots.'

'Pure professional jealousy, in fact?'

'Yes, and I suppose it was a sort of loyalty on Sven's part which made him spin you such a yarn. Also it would appeal to his romantic nature that one of his colleagues should have been martyred for his political opinions, rather than for causing the death of an innocent youth through sheer carelessness.'

'I'm still not entirely convinced that it was sheer carelessness. Apart from the spy thing, he could have had some other motive. Furthermore, I don't recall that his movements were ever properly accounted for at the time of Mrs Baker's murder. His wife says he joined her in the main hall at the time they had arranged, and he is presumed to have been in his office up to that point, but so far as I know we only have their word for it.'

'No, there have been many more words for it than that, I assure you. But I can't go into it now, can I? Terrible Pierre will be here at any moment and I still have some packing to finish.'

*

This conversation sent the pendulum swinging over to the other side again and, instead of applying myself to my own business when Robin and Ellen had left, I gathered up the pages of 'The Waiting Room', and the menu card from the Auberge du Père Bernard, and seated myself at the desk for a spell of concentrated thought.

However, I had reckoned without Lupe and her passionate though somewhat unco-ordinated approach to housework. So long as I sat in my bedroom, it seemed that the only patch she needed to clean was around my feet. When I escaped to Ellen's room I found that the bed had been stripped off to air, and all the blankets and sheets draped over the rest of the furniture. In the salon the rugs had been rolled back and chairs stacked on to tables, in readiness for floor polishing. In desperation, I crept into the bathroom, meaning to recline in the tub for a bit, and had craftily locked myself in before discovering that it was half filled with soapy water and Robin's shirts and socks. I could not even steady my jangling nerves with a cigarette, because she had removed all the ashtrays and plunged them into the kitchen sink.

The only solution was to seek refuge outside and I blessed the benevolent French custom of providing the freedom of a table and chair, plus indefinite shelter from the storm, in return for the price of a cup of coffee.

I had intended to go no further than the brasserie opposite the flat, but changed course as I was crossing the road. Mademoiselle Pêche was already installed there, with her sandwich and carafe, proving that she was either a very persistent trier, or that I had been wrong about her motives in the first place.

I made a diagonal crossing and turned into the Champ de Mars, hoping that its ambience might stimulate inspiration. This it signally failed to do, and when I emerged at the exit by the Avenue du Bourdonnais I was no nearer solving any of the puzzles which I was beginning to fear would stand forever between me and my work unless I could get them untangled.

Things took a turn for the better when I seated myself at a table in the café where Robin and I had forced our company on the unwilling Reg Baker. Reminders popped up all around and ideas soon began to flow from them. I was served by the same waiter as before and this time I noticed that he was wearing a heavy gold signet ring. Well-dressed women, dragging poodles, shuffled past me in their dozens, and when I glanced up at the Ecole Militaire I saw four pigeons pecking and preening on the gravel forecourt.

Furthermore, I even caught a glimpse of Mr Baker, and guessed that he had also caught a glimpse of me, for he had threaded his way through the pavement tables and was almost up to the door, when he reacted in precisely the same way as I had at the sight of Miss Pêche. He hesitated, then wheeled off in the opposite direction and walked rapidly away.

All these memory-jerkers had their effect and, two coffees and forty minutes later, the light at the end of the tunnel was beginning to burn with a reasonably cheerful glow. The next task was to formulate a programme to carry me on to stage two and it finally resolved itself into three separate projects of varying degrees of trickiness: to make another appointment with Mireille; to ascertain the licence number of one particular car; and to invent a plausible excuse for another meeting with Adela, preferably in her own house.

The first and technically the simplest of these could not be accomplished until the following day, when the hair-dresser's reopened, but I had already set some mental wheels in motion for the other two.

I was so elated by the progress I had made and so engrossed in plans to extend it that I lavishly overtipped the waiter and then stood up, leaving my bag unfastened. He must have been bracing himself for something of this kind, for he sprang forward, wagged his finger at me and launched into a lecture about the many naughty people who would not scruple to profit by my carelessness.

I felt profoundly grateful to him, but realised I should have to stop going there, as I was really beginning to scare him to death.

(ii)

I treated myself to lunch at a restaurant, partly to indulge my self-satisfied mood and partly to avoid further skirmishes with Lupe, should she still be rampaging round the flat. It was after two when I got back there and the place was deserted, with no crease or speck to show that it had ever been inhabited. However, the implications of this had barely impinged when the telephone rang.

It was Robin on the line and he used the brisk, rather remote tone of voice which I associated with preoccupation in matters relating to the criminal classes.

'Where on earth have you been, Tessa? Listen, I'm coming back to Paris. I thought I'd better warn you.'

'What's happened? Another late arrival of the incoming aircraft?'

'No. I can't explain over the telephone, but I've just had some information which makes it necessary to stop on for a bit.'

'I'm delighted to hear it. And all is now revealed.'

'Is it?' he asked, descending from his high horse. 'What is revealed?'

'Why Ellen isn't back. I was about to start sending cables and now I needn't bother.'

Instead of his confirming this, there was silence and I thought we had been cut off.

'Robin! Are you still there?'

'Yes, I'm here. Now listen, don't flap. I'm positive she'll be back in a moment, but in point of fact she left here just after one o'clock.'

'But that's over an hour ago. It shouldn't take more than twenty-five minutes, at this time of day.'

'Nearer forty.'

'Nevertheless. Did you actually see her leave?'

'No, but Pierre was waiting for her and we'd arranged what time and all that. It's bound to be all right. I expect she came in, found you weren't there and went out again. Yes, that's obviously what happened.'

'No, it obviously isn't,' I told him. 'I've looked in her bedroom and one thing is definite. She hasn't set foot there since Lupe left.'

'Okay, so she got Pierre to drop her off at Saint Germain or somewhere, instead of coming straight home. Nothing to worry about.'

'Oh, Robin, she wouldn't do that without letting me know. Would she?'

'Do try to keep calm. I'm sure there's a very simple explanation, but if she hasn't turned up by the time I arrive I promise to organise a search party.'

'All right, but do hurry! No, no! What am I saying?'

'I'm not clairvoyant. What are you saying?'

'Please do not hurry. Make your taxi go very very slowly. I've seen too many pile-ups on that ghastly auto-route. Oh, Robin, you don't think that's what Ellen . . . ?'

'No, of course not. Pierre's a most careful driver. Just keep calm and try to contain yourself until I get back.'

'All right,' I agreed, resisting the insane impulse to beg him to be quick about it.

It was only when he had rung off that it struck me that I had not asked him about the nature of the business which was bringing him back to Paris; but the thought was immediately crowded out by others, more pressing, and I returned for another inspection of Ellen's room. Even the record player was closed and the records neatly stacked, a sure sign that she had not spent two minutes there in the recent past.

Irrespective of my commands and countermands, I knew that I had another half hour to wait, before stationing myself at the window to watch for Robin's arrival. I decided to spend them in my bedroom, so as to pounce on the telephone the moment it rang.

I went over to the desk, where I had thrown down the script and menu card, meaning to lock them away in one of the drawers. It was while stooping down to do this that my eye was caught by something out of place. Lying all by itself in the scrubbed and polished waste-paper basket was a crumpled wodge of paper, the size of a tennis ball.

The significance did not immediately strike me. When it did, I dipped my hand in the basket, the blood pounding so furiously in my ears that I almost lost my balance and toppled out of the chair.

I unrolled the ball and smoothed it out on the blotter. There was an envelope addressed simply: 'Ellen', and one sheet of paper. They were both of the brand called 'Bonde Parisien', of which there were several pads in the flat, and doubtless in half the other flats of Paris. The message was as follows:

Drop everything, hop in a taxi and meet me at Fouquet's. Something exciting has turned up and no time to be lost. Explain when I see you. Love, T.

(iii)

'It's not my writing,' I told Robin. 'You do realise that?'

'It's not even particularly like your writing. The mystery is that Ellen should have been fooled by it.'

'There's a reason for that. It's not so unlike the way I wrote when my hand was bound up.'

'Where do you suppose she found it?'

'Downstairs in our mail-box, presumably. I expect she wanted to go to the bathroom and came upstairs to read it. That would account for her being in my bedroom.'

'Well, try not to worry. It's probably just someone having a joke. Jonathan, most likely. Has her cap gone too, by the way?'

Despite his assurances, I could tell that he was a mite worried himself, and when I informed him that the cap was not in the flat he made two telephone calls. The first was to Fouquet's, but no one answering Ellen's description or wearing her distinctive headgear had been seen there. The second was to someone at the Sûreté. The whole performance took no more than seven or eight minutes, but I was in a frenzy of impatience, lest Ellen should be trying to telephone us.

'I'll go down there myself, presently,' Robin said, referring to his second call. 'I can probably stir them up a bit quicker in that way, but first of all I want to get a few things sorted out. Assuming for the moment that it isn't some feeble joke, who is there in Paris who has seen your handwriting? Lupe?'

'Well, yes, I've left her shopping lists and so on; but you can't seriously suspect Lupe, Robin. She hardly speaks a word of English, certainly not enough to have written that foul note.'

'We can't exclude anyone at the moment. Who else?'

'Practically everyone,' I admitted hopelessly. 'The Müllers, for a start. You made me write that note about the hairdresser.'

'How about Jonathan? I still think he's probably at the bottom of it. I daresay he wanted to see Ellen and was afraid she would refuse, after his tiresome behaviour yesterday.'

'In a way, he's had more opportunities than anyone. He delivered a note for Adela and he could also have seen the one which Ellen posted to Mrs Müller. That applies to Pêche, too. She was nosing through my desk and the letter was lying there, in full view.'

'Anyone else?'

'Yes, there's Adela. The only thing is that I wrote to her before I got bitten by the hysterical poodle, so she ought to have made a better job of it. And, if you include Adela, you must put in Reg Baker, as well, because I bet she showed him my letter.'

'And that's the lot?'

'No, there's still Sven. He got a fine specimen off me, much more like this forgery than the real thing, because I was worried and bemused, not to mention slightly high, when I scribbled down our address at the airport. But still, he's the one person we can rule out.'

Robin looked down at his shoes and then up again:

'No, we can't, Tessa.'

'Oh, come now! Seeing he's safely behind bars.'

'Not any more. As from ten this morning, he's a free man.'

'You're joking?'

'No, I'm not. There've been what we call fresh developments. They're the reason for my being here now, instead of winging back to London.'

'Oh God, yes, I completely forgot to ask you about that. I'm terribly sorry, Robin, but this worry over Ellen has pushed everything else out of my mind.'

'Which is only natural. In fact, I wouldn't have mentioned the other thing, except that it might have some bearing on Ellen's disappearance.'

'What happened, then? Has Sven escaped?'

'No, he's been released. They've dropped the charges.'

'You don't mean to tell me he's been able to prove he was in the cinema, after all?'

'No, he's been supplanted. Someone else has confessed.'

'Are you serious? Is it . . . ?'

'Dr Müller.'

'No! Are you sure, Robin? I can hardly believe it. You mean, he's actually confessed? Why did he kill her?'

'No idea. I haven't even seen the letter yet.'

'Oh,' I said slowly. 'You mean he's dead?'

'Last night, at that place of theirs in the country. Died in his sleep from an overdose. The police had already rung up and asked him to call first thing this morning when he got back to Paris, so I suppose he thought the game was up. Naturally, he knew just the right stuff to knock himself out with, so it was all over before anyone found him.'

'How very obliging of him! And I suppose they found a suicide note and full confession, all neatly typed out and lying on his bedside table? Who else was at their house last night? Adela for one, and Reg Baker too, if my deductions are correct.'

'Also Mademoiselle Pêche, strangely enough,' Robin said.

'You don't say?'

'Apparently, she's the go-between for Adela and Sven's solicitor. Adela got her down there yesterday for consultations and she stayed the night.'

'How very interesting! And I think I can add another to the list. Although he may not have been in at the death, so to speak.'

'Who's that?'

'Look at this,' I said, getting up and fetching the menu card. 'Take a look at that map and, considering what happened yesterday, you'll see what I mean.'

'You may be right,' he agreed, when he had studied it. 'I'll do a check.'

'But meanwhile all we know for certain is that Sven's on the loose again?'

'Yes, awkward of him, isn't it? Things have been comparatively quiet since they locked him up, and now we have this new complication. Could it be another of his pranks?'

'Somehow, I don't think so. I agree there are certain features which make one think of him, but I also believe that he's fundamentally kind. I don't think he'd behave in a cruel way. Oh, I'd do anything if she'd only come walking in! You don't think I ought to let Toby know, do you?'

'Absolutely not. He's at sea, for one thing. Even if we did get a message to him, there's nothing he could do about it until the boat docks, and we'll have it all cleared up long before that. If she's not with Jonathan, listening to records somewhere, as I strongly suspect, the police are bound to catch up with her pretty soon. They're frightfully efficient.'

'I admire your faith,' I said, 'but they might work faster still with a little prodding. I honestly think it's time you went down there and gave them a shove.'

'I'm on my way,' he said, tearing a page from his diary and handing it to me. 'You'd better stick around for the telephone. I'll be in touch anyway, but you can call me at this number and extension, if you get any news.'

He had reached the door and was going out, when he hesitated, then stopped and turned round again, a faintly puzzled expression on his face.

'There's just one thing, Tessa.'

'Yes?'

'Well, of course I realise you're far too anxious about Ellen to give much attention to other things, but . . .'

'Yes?' I said again, endeavouring to conceal my impatience.

'It's just that you seemed to be knocked all of a heap when I told you Müller had confessed. On the other hand, you didn't show any surprise at all to learn that he had killed himself.'

I am inclined to believe that I shall be unable to resist a curtain line, even on my death-bed. I said:

'Oh, I wasn't. Not in the least. The only surprise is that it's happened so soon.'

(iv)

I do not know whether Robin had believed there was the slightest danger of my moving more than two feet away from the telephone, but I could just as well have gone out and danced on the tables of Montmartre, for all the good my vigilance did me. There was no word from Ellen, nor any development at all on that front. Robin, himself, gave me a couple of heart attacks by ringing up to report on which steps were being taken by whom, but when it was boiled down, the news from that quarter also amounted to nothing at all.

I kept the radio humming away, in case there should be a news flash, but this brought no results either, and I understood why when Robin returned, just as I lowered the volume again after the six o'clock bulletin. He told me that the police were withholding all information from the Press, until it was felt that their co-operation might prove valuable, and in the meantime were keeping their activities secret. This was not a policy which had my unqualified vote.

'That's all very well,' I complained, 'but if it's ransom they want, I should like every paper to carry the front page news that we're willing to pay whatever the kidnappers demand.'

'Only we don't believe for one moment that it is ransom, do we?'

'It has happened before.'

'Oh yes, if we were Rothschilds or something, but this is another kind of blackmail. If she has been kidnapped, it's because there's something they want from us, but I don't believe it's money.'

'No,' I admitted, 'perhaps not, but by playing it this way we have absolutely no means of finding out what they do want.'

'We'll know,' he said grimly, 'just as soon as they're ready to tell us.'

He was right, as usual, though I had almost despaired of it when the call came through, nearly four hours later.

We were facing each other on the twin beds, pretending to concentrate on a game of scrabble, with the telephone on the table between us. When it rang I experienced five seconds of total paralysis, before diving at it with both hands. In one movement, I grabbed the receiver, unhooked the extra earpiece and handed it to Robin. A voice said in French:

'Are you there, Mrs Price?'

'Yes, I'm listening. Is Ellen there?'

'No questions, please. Your cousin is safe. She will be returned to you as soon as certain conditions have been fulfilled, and have been seen to be fulfilled.'

I glanced up at Robin. There was a score card among the scattered scrabble pieces and he had already made some notes on it.

'Did you hear me?' the voice asked.

'Oui.'

'You may speak in English. I know well that you can understand some French, but if there is anything not perfectly clear, you are to ask me. Understood?'

'Yes.'

'Listen, then. You are to make all arrangements to leave Paris immediately.'

'But . . .'

'Shut up and listen. Tomorrow morning you will receive through the post a doctor's certificate, stating that you suffer from acute appendicitis, which makes it necessary for an operation within twenty-four hours.'

'But . . .'

'Do not interrupt. You will then telephone to your doctor in London, so that he may arrange for you to be met on arrival and taken directly to a nursing-home. Your arrival time at Heathrow is four-fifty. You had better write that down.'

I waited while Robin did so, then said: 'Yes, go on.'

'You will then speak with your agent and instruct him to contact the Paris studios, to explain that you must cancel your contract with them. Is this fully understood?'

'Oh yes, but . . .'

'I shall continue then. You will send your maid with a letter and five hundred francs to Cook's Bureau in the Place de la Madeleine, and you will also enclose your cousin's passport. You will instruct them to hand over one first-class single ticket, which they are holding in your name, for Air France flight leaving Orly at four o'clock. You will also say in your letter that your cousin's passport and the other ticket, which has been booked in her name, will be collected by a separate messenger. Is this clear?'

'Yes.'

'At two forty-five a car will call at your flat to take you in the airport. You are feeling ill, so you do not speak to the driver. You will have the doctor's certificate with you, to make sure there are no delays, but the airport officials will be expecting you. There will be an invalid chair and attendant to take you directly to the aircraft. That is all.'

'But what about Ellen?'

'If you have followed these instructions exactly, your cousin will meet you on the plane with the other passengers. Have you understood?'

'Yes.'

'Good. So there is a final warning. You are not to speak to anyone, now or later, of some events which have occurred while you were in Paris. If you disobey this order, it will be known at once and you or one of your family will suffer.'

The voice ceased. There was a click and I found myself listening stupidly to the whine of the dialling tone.

'It's insane,' I said, staring wildly at Robin. 'I'm going crazy. This can't be happening.'

He took the receiver from my hand, rested it on the bar for a few seconds and then lifted it again.

'What are you doing?' I screamed, snatching it out of his hand.

'Reporting to the Sûreté, of course. What else?'

'No, no, you mustn't. Listen, Robin, have you gone crazy, too? Don't you realise that if we breathe a word of this, they'll find out and do something terrible to Ellen? I know they will. I believed every word that voice was saying, didn't you?'

'The point is that we can't possibly expect much help from the police, unless we co-operate with them every step of the way.'

'But we don't really need their help now, do we? Not just at the moment anyway. What I mean is, we've achieved something concrete at last. For God's sake, let's not throw it away until we have something equally good to put in its place. Well, do at any rate talk it over before you make some move which might destroy everything.'

'Very well,' he said, replacing the receiver, 'but I still think my way is the right one. And what is there to talk about?'

'Well, for one thing, did you have any ideas about who that voice belonged to?'

'No. Not a Frenchwoman, obviously. The accent was quite strong. Could have been English.'

'On the other hand, it could have been a Frenchwoman who mixes a lot with foreigners and can imitate different accents?'

'I suppose so.'

'Are we even safe in assuming it was a woman?'

'We're not safe in assuming anything. That's why I think your decision to play a lone hand is such a mistake. We oughtn't to lose a minute before bringing in the experts. If the call came from outside Paris, there might be a chance they could trace it.'

'Yes, and then the gang would find out the police were on their trail and probably kill Ellen out of revenge. They wouldn't have much to lose.'

'In other words, you mean to follow their instructions, go through with the whole programme and say nothing to anybody?'

'Unless we can find an alternative which won't endanger Ellen, yes I do.'

'It won't help your career much, you know; or mine, either.'

'Oh, Robin, how could we possibly bother about any of that?'

'I suppose not, but it's still a gamble. This could be a hoax, you know. It could also be bluff. Someone might know that Ellen was away on some perfectly innocent jaunt and was using their knowledge to trick you into leaving the country. I would put that high on the list of probabilities.'

'Why?'

'Because if they really had their claws on her, I would expect them to be a little more accurate in their information. Even you must have noticed one or two undeliberate mistakes. How about your suddenly developing acute appendicitis, you who had it whipped out when you were five years old? Everyone who knows you well has heard that pathetic tale more than once and I bet Ellen was no exception.'

'It's true; and I also noticed that they're not aware that you've doubled back to Paris, though I fail to see how it can help us in any way.'

'It may yet do so, but I was thinking more in terms of what Ellen would have been able to tell them.'

'Like their referring to my agent as though she were a man? I know, but it doesn't prove they haven't got her in their clutches. She could have been drugged.'

'More than likely. Nevertheless, it would have been only prudent to have got as much information as possible out of her, first.'

'It was as though someone were reading a part, or had learnt it by heart and could only get through to the end, so long as there were no interruptions or unrehearsed questions.'

'I'm thankful they didn't allow you to break the flow, though, Tessa. It might have ended with their discovering how little you actually do know about Leila Baker's murder. There's no telling how they might have reacted, on finding that all their trouble had been for nothing. That is, assuming that this is a genuine kidnap and the two things are connected.'

I was rather at a loss for a reply to this, but since it had been framed as a statement and not a question I let it go by and asked: 'Why is that supposed to be an advantage?'

'Because the less they know, the stronger it makes our hand. I was puzzled at first by this touching belief that you knew something which would put them in jeopardy, but I think I've hit on the answer now.'

'Oh? What's that?'

'Jonathan. One has to remember that his kind of fantasy boasting invariably works in both directions. He brags to Ellen about his fairy-tale life in the States, and no doubt he brags just as much about her, to everyone else. Can't you just hear the stories that are put around about her cousin who is such a celebrated actress, and at the same time such a master mind that she is called in to assist Scotland Yard with all their most baffling cases?'

'I only hope you're right, Robin, and that's all it is. Personally, I've got this grinding fear that it's Ellen who possesses the one bit of knowledge which could put a spanner in their works. If so, I just pray she'll keep her mouth shut.'

'What bit of knowledge?'

'Oh, simply that the alibis for Mrs Baker's murder are only half the story. It would be just as important to know what all our suspects were doing when old Vishna died. I think Ellen has grasped that, and I do so wish I'd thrashed it out with her, instead of trying to bury it out of sight.'

'I wish you'd tell me what you're on about, Tessa?'

So I reminded him of Ellen's remark when we were leaving the concert and how it tied in with Mrs Baker's distraught mood when I met her a few days later.

'I shouldn't worry too much about that,' he said. 'Ellen is rather given to dramatic pronouncements and I daresay this was just such another. Even if it did have some factual basis, nothing could ever be proved, one way or the other. The old man's body was flown home the very next morning and we know what happens to Hindus when they die. So whatever Ellen saw, or imagined she saw, she's no real danger to them. I think you're the one they're scared of and my own hunch is that Jonathan's to blame for that. It would never surprise me if he claimed you had actually solved the case. Very childish, of course, but you never know whose guilty conscience may have been at work to persuade someone it was true.'

'It's not all that childish, though, Robin. The fact is that I really have come up with some theories about the murder and, what's more, I think they provide the answer. I had meant to tell you about it, naturally, but I only hit on the solution today, and now this business of Ellen has changed everything. The trouble is, you see, that I have none of what the police would call proof. The best that could happen, if they took me seriously, is that they'd go dumping off in all directions, hammering on doors and asking a lot of more or less pertinent questions. The murderer would get the wind up, guess who was responsible and probably take it out on Ellen. I couldn't risk it.'

'I haven't the least idea what you're talking about,' Robin said, 'but obviously it doesn't include the concept of Dr Müller as the murderer.'

'No, and I can't believe that you include it, either; not after that telephone call. That made it quite clear that the murderer is still very much alive. However, I'm all for letting them believe they've fooled everyone with Dr Müller's fake suicide, at any rate until Ellen is safely back. After that, if they've kept their word, I shan't care what happens. They can wipe out half the population of France before they'll hear a squeak out of me.'

Robin was looking thoughtful: 'All the same, Tess, I think you should tell me a little about these inflammable theories. It's just possible they could point to a way of getting Ellen safely back, without quite such drastic consequences.'

'And I know you'd be the one to find it,' I said, 'but I'll only tell you if you give your solemn word not to pass it on to the police.'

'You have my solemn word,' he replied.

So then I told him, and he looked more thoughtful than ever.

(v)

In asserting so positively that breaking my contract was a mere triviality in this crisis, I had been a little less than frank and quite a lot holier than me. The truth was that, had I still possessed a heart to be broken, this would have been the thing to do it, and the unforeseen patience and friendliness which, from the producer downwards, they had all shown me made it even harder to bear. The thought of all the trouble and expense I should be putting them to was a bitter pill and the fact that I should have felt almost as treacherous if my non-existent appendix had really been to blame was no consolation at all.

None of this altered by one jot the conviction that Ellen's safety was the vital factor, but it did add the last small drop to my sadness and sense of failure. No doubt sensing this, Robin advised me to relax and get a few hours'

172 | ANNE MORICE

sleep. I protested that I not only could not, but would not contemplate such a thing. To indulge myself in that way, with Ellen alone and possibly scared, would have been the worst betrayal of all. He refrained from pointing out that lying awake all night would bring no comfort to her, but patiently suggested that I should need all my wits about me the following day, when a little quick thinking might prove crucial. This was unanswerable and I compromised by saying that I would lie down for a few hours, though confident I should never be able to close my eyes. With a little help from Jonathan, I almost managed not to.

It was around one o'clock when the doorbell rang. Robin turned over, swearing as he woke, then sat bolt upright; but I was halfway across the room by that time, heading for the hall.

When I saw him through the peephole, I was tempted to creep away and leave him there, but he looked so wild and farouche, with a red scratch down one side of his face and red blotches on the other, that I was afraid he might alarm the neighbours by trying to break the door down.

'Where's Ellie?' he demanded, in his usual pretty way, as I opened the door.

'Not here. Did you expect her to be?'

'Where is she?'

'I was hoping you might tell me. You'd better come inside before we wake the whole building. It's long past midnight, in case you didn't know.'

He followed me into the salon and pushed some of the hair out of his eyes.

'Where is she?' he said again.

'We don't know. I thought I'd made that clear. I'll explain in a minute, but first I want to hear a few things from you.

When did you last see or speak to Ellen, and where was she at the time?'

Robin joined us at this point and took over the interrogation. In his expert hands, even the mulish Jonathan became as putty, and we got the whole story in under half an hour. The fact that it added nothing relevant to what we already knew did not lessen the achievement.

He told us that he had spent the night alone in the Rue des Quatre Pigeons and, having overslept, was awakened by his stepfather arriving home in a taxi. Not wishing for a confrontation, he had pulled the bedclothes over his head. A short while later he had heard the front door slam and had nipped out of bed and over to the window, just in time to see Sven crossing the courtyard, with a small suitcase in his hand.

He had then dressed and made himself some breakfast, and while eating it had tried to telephone Ellen; but Lupe had answered and he couldn't get any sense out of her.

Unaware that Ellen had gone to the airport, he had set off in search of her, in drug-stores and various other haunts which they both frequented. During this odyssey he had tried a couple more times to call our number, but there was no reply. Concluding, with sublime egocentricity, that the only conceivable reason for this was that Ellen was trying to avoid him, he had become deeply depressed. Moreover, at various stops along the way he had paused to down a reviving rum and Coca-Cola. At his last port of call he had run into some acquaintances, who, hearing of his plight, had endeavoured to cheer him up with several more of the same.

Since it was by then late afternoon and he had eaten nothing but a few spoonfuls of cereal since the previous evening, he began to feel somewhat peculiar and had eventually weaved his way back to the Quatre Pigeons, more or less stoned.

On arrival, he found that his mother had returned from the country and was in a flat spin about something or other, although he hadn't the energy to find out what it was. When she saw the condition he was in she became more incensed than ever and had commanded him to go soak his head in cold water; but he had explained that he first of all had to make an urgent telephone call to his friend Ellie. Whereupon she had struck him across the face and locked him in the bathroom, where he had promptly passed out on the floor.

He could not tell what time it was when he came to because his watch had stopped, but it was already dark. He strained his ears, but could hear no sound at all, not even the dogs yapping, and concluded that he was alone in the flat. Stiff as a board and drenched in self-pity, with a splitting head, he had lain for some while hopeless and inert on the floor. Then he remembered that the bathroom cupboard contained cures for at least some of his ills and he had got up and mixed himself a fizzy drink. This so far revived him that he was able to take stock of his situation and formulate plans for getting out of it.

The window was high up and tiny, but the bathroom was on the ground flowed he reckoned that if he could squeeze through he would only have a few feet to fall. He managed to break the glass with a tin of scouring powder, but did not make a very neat job of it, leaving a jagged rim round the frame, which he could not gouge out, and on the first attempt to crawl through had scratched his face. It was not a deep cut, but it bled ferociously and so he had to retreat inside again, to mop himself up and apply disinfectant. He had wrapped his head in a bath-towel for the second attempt, and this one was successful.

It was only after he had picked himself up, crammed the towel back through the window and was making for the street that he realised that the afternoon's debauchery had cleaned him out, and that he did not even possess the price of a telephone call. It also dawned on him that he was mad with hunger.

Moody, but still not entirely bowed, he had trudged off towards the centre of Paris, then over a bridge to the Left Bank. He had staggered round in the area of Boulevard St Michel for what seemed like hours, scanning the bars and cafés as he went. The quest this time was not rum and coke, but any sympathetic acquaintance who might be prevailed upon to underwrite him for a sandwich and a métro ticket, if not a bed for the night, but it met with no success.

I considered that, even allowing for a little exaggeration, this saga showed a lot more guts and enterprise than I had formerly associated with Jonathan, and at this point in the narrative I left the room to knock up some bacon and eggs. So I missed the concluding paragraphs, which Robin told me later amounted to little more than that, catching sight of the Sorbonne clock and finding it was past midnight, he had decided to throw himself on our mercy. To which end he had slogged the two miles over to Suffren.

Robin was doing the talking when I returned and, watching Jonathan intently as he waded into the bacon and eggs, he gave him a factual account of Ellen's kidnapping, plus the conditions which had been imposed for her release.

It was difficult to judge Jonathan's reactions, because he kept his head bent over the plate and his hair hung forward, shielding his face like a thick black curtain. It was noticeable, however, that his ravenous appetite was soon sated and after a while he abandoned the pretence of eating and pushed the tray aside. If Robin noticed it, too, he ignored it and launched into a brief account of Dr Müller's suicide. He added that it was doubtless the shock and distress brought on by this event which had caused Adela to behave so harshly. I imagine that his move in putting all these cards on the table was to jerk some response out of Jonathan, which would reveal whether or not he knew more about Ellen's disappearance than he pretended; but, if so, it failed completely, for he did not utter a word.

Probably the most practical thing would have been to give him Ellen's room, but this would have been tantamount to admitting that I had abandoned all hope of her returning that night and this, although dawn was only a few hours away, I obstinately refused to do. So we got out all the pillows and wraps which Lupe had tidied away, and once more went through the laborious process of making up a bed on the floor. Jonathan made no attempt to help us, but sat like a lump on the sofa, legs apart, elbows on knees, and his chin cupped in his hands, still in stony silence.

'Poor chap's completely whacked,' Robin said indulgently, when we were back in our own room. 'He doesn't know whether he's coming or going.'

He wasn't the only one. I flopped on my bed, checked with my travelling clock on the number of hours still to be got through before daylight, and in two minutes was fast asleep.

ELEVEN

I COULD tell by the level of the sun streaming in at the window that it was around eight o'clock when I woke up, and I lay still for a few more minutes, wondering what it was that I was so unhappy about. When I had got that sorted out, I rose and began to attend to some of the rest. There was oceans of time because Lupe was not due for another two hours, but any activity was preferable to wilting away under the sickening sense of defeat and apprehension.

I found both passports and put Ellen's in an envelope, with a covering note addressed to Cook's. The only thing needed before sealing it down was five hundred francs in cash, and I found that my purse did not contain even half this amount. Robin was still asleep and it would have been pointless to wake him, for he had unloaded practically all his French money on to me, before leaving for the airport.

This small setback, coming so early in the proceedings, almost threw me, for there is nothing a French bank hates so much as parting with cash. There was little chance of their doing so, were Lupe to present my cheque, and with my acute appendicitis I could hardly take it to them in person. Luckily, just before the last frail thread of self-control snapped in two, I recollected the emergency hoard in the sideboard drawer.

For purposes of burglar thwarting, it was kept in a chocolate box among the packs of cards and scrabble board, and except at weekends when we regularly exceeded our budget, it normally contained a fairly tidy sum.

In my impatience to get at it, I had no compunction in disturbing Jonathan, which was just as well because when I entered the salon he was not there.

It was a grisly scene, with the plate of congealed bacon and eggs still on the table, and the pillows and sheets, my velvet wrap and a pair of Robin's pyjamas all scrumpled up together on the floor. I turned my back on it and concentrated on the sideboard. The chocolate box was in place and also the notebook in which I methodically entered each deposit and withdrawal. I do not quite know why I did this, except that it made me feel businesslike and efficient, but I was apt to be fanatical about it. On this occasion the system paid off, in a sense, because only a glance was needed to show that the box should have contained four hundred and three francs; and a second one brought the news that it actually contained precisely two hundred.

'Does Lupe know where you keep it?' Robin asked, when I had stumbled back to the bedroom to apprise him of this outrage.

'Of course she does. She uses it for the shopping, but she always gives me an account of every penny. Ellen does the same. They both know all about my obsession. You know what I think?'

'No, what?'

'I think that fiendish little Jonathan took it.'

'Oh, would he do a thing like that?'

'You bet he would. I expect he's seen Ellen taking money for the movies and so on, and he told us himself he was cleaned out.'

'Well, if he did borrow it, I'm sure he'll bring it back as soon as the banks open.'

Privately, I was of the opinion that he was more likely to squander the lot on rum and coke, but fortunately the situation was not desperate. Robin unearthed a fifty-franc note, which he had kept back for the duty-free shop, and by pooling our resources we were able to scrape up the required amount, with exactly two francs over. If the driver or wheel-chair attendant expected a tip, it was going to be just too bad.

Lupe arrived punctually, and with her the last faint hope of waking from this nightmare oozed away. She had found only one letter in our box and it contained the doctor's certificate. The practitioner's name, Dr Mathieu Baudouin, was printed at the top, over an address in Neuilly, and the typed message declared that, in the opinion of the sous-signé, the patient was unfit for work and in need of urgent surgical attention. As a matter of fact, the sous-signature consisted of three dashes, two vertical and one horizontal, but perhaps legibility in that context would have been even more suspect.

I gave Lupe the Cook's envelope and, on Robin's advice, explained that I was obliged to go to London for a few days, for health reasons, but that we wished her to carry on as usual, since Monsieur would remain in residence. Her obstetrical obsessions came in handy at this point, because she immediately began to treat me with the veneration usually reserved for the Virgin Mary, and thereafter tumbled over herself to gratify my every whim.

'Did you remember to tell the office downstairs that we had changed the locks?' Robin asked, when she had departed.

'No. At least, I did try once, but there was no one there and then I forgot all about it. Is it important?'

'Very.'

'Oh Lord! I'm awfully sorry. What can I do?'

'Very important indeed,' he said, giving me a hug. 'In fact, it's the most constructive bit of forgetting you've ever done. Now, come on, what about those telephone calls? It would be best to appear to be doing everything according to the book.'

'Not just appear to; actually do so.'

'Well yes, that may apply to you, but I consider myself a relatively free agent.'

'Very relative, remembering your solemn oath. You're not up to anything, are you?'

'No, you'll be relieved to hear that my policy is to keep well in the background. I still feel that we have a slight edge in that they don't know I'm in Paris and that we might somehow turn it to our advantage.'

'Very well, I've no objection to that,' I said, picking up the telephone, to put those clogged wheels in motion for a call to London.

The difficulties proved surmountable for once, and I had two unforeseen strokes of luck, as a bonus. My agent was so flabbergasted by my request and so choked with rage by my refusal to spend a couple of nights at the Anglo-American hospital and get the whole matter tidied up with a few injections that after the initial outburst she could hardly bring herself to speak at all. Had my life really been in danger from acute appendicitis, I might have found her attitude a trifle heartless, but as it was I could only be grateful for her brief and surly responses.

By the time I got through to my doctor's number, he was out on his calls, so all I had to do was spell out the message to his secretary. Not a word had been spoken by anyone concerned which could not safely have been overheard by the enemy.

'Listen now, Tessa,' Robin said, when I had concluded this dreary farce. 'There are two things I want you to do. When the time comes, I think you should let Lupe carry your suitcase down to the car.'

'Only one case for all this lot?' I asked, gazing helplessly at my mountain of possessions.

'Yes, I think so. In the first place, you've told her that it's only for a few days and we want to keep that pretence going. Also it would look more authentic to any watchers who may be hanging around. You're supposed to be at death's door and in no condition to pack ten or twelve cases. The natural thing would be to have the bulk of it sent on after you.'

'Okay. What else?'

'At some point during the morning, I want you to tell Lupe that you're going to leave her the old set of keys, so that she can return them to the office, some time or other. You can be quite casual about it and not refer to it again until you are actually getting in the car. If she reminds you, herself, at this point, so much the better. The important thing is for the driver to see you hand her a bunch of keys. Got it?'

'In one. You're brilliant.'

'Thanks. With any luck, their interest in this flat will cease, once you've left on schedule. If we should get any kind of a break, or if anything were to go wrong, at least I'll be here and able to take it up from that point.'

'By anything going wrong, I suppose you mean they might double-cross me and not get Ellen to the plane at all.'

'It's unlikely, but it has to be taken into account.'

'Not by me,' I told him firmly. 'I mean to tell myself with every breath I draw that she will be there; that she'll come bouncing on with all flags flying and this nightmare will be over. How else could I get through it? And you believe it, too, don't you, Robin?'

'Yes,' he said, 'I do. With all my heart.'

Nothing was to turn out quite as we both pretended to be so confident in predicting, but at least his assurance gave me the courage to complete the preliminary stages without faltering, and at twenty minutes to three, wrapped in a fur coat and leaning on Lupe's arm, I went downstairs to the waiting car.

(ii)

The driver was a rat-faced, surly little man, very different from spirited old Pierre, with dark hair and complexion.
He did not stir from his seat or attempt to open the door
when Lupe handed me in, and although we managed the
business with the keys exactly according to plan, I had the
sensation that we were playing to an empty house. Not a
ripple of curiosity disturbed his sour expression, and when
Lupe stood back and waved goodbye, the tears pouring down
her face, he ignored her completely, slammed the car into
gear and shot away from the pavement. As it happens, I
think they were tears of joy for the impending happy event,
rather than that other brand of sweet sorrow, but the sight
of them was not much of a backbone stiffener.

In one respect, it was a relief to be in the company of
this callous individual, for I find it hard to ignore friendly
overtures, from whatever source, and I saw that I should
have no problem over that part of the instructions which
forbade communication with the driver. However, I could
not tell how much he might be observing, and it behoved
me to be cautious. At one point we halted at some traffic
lights, before turning into the Boulevard de Grenelle, and
I glanced up at the rear mirror and saw his eyes, insolent
and inimical, fixed steadily upon me. Apart from anything
else, I did not consider this to be quite the safest way to
drive through Paris and, to discourage it, pulled my collar
up round my face, leant back against the cushion which
Lupe had provided and closed my eyes.

This meant that I could only guess at our rate of progress, but the route had become moderately familiar and, by
exerting all the other senses to their full capacity, I could
trace most of it in my head. There was the usual long hold
up at the Porte de Versailles, followed soon afterwards by

the even longer one as we edged towards the peripheral road at Montrouge. Once through this, we put on a good spurt and, almost before I was ready for it, I could hear the muffled swishing sound which indicated that we were circling the tunnel leading to the auto-route proper.

The longest part of the journey, in time if not distance, was now behind us and the remainder should have been plain sailing, as indeed, for the first few miles, it was. Then, unaccountably, we slowed down, limped forward a few yards, crawled again and finally stopped. Nothing whatever happened and a blinding sense of fear and frustration took hold of me. All at once it struck me that I had been tricked into making this preposterous journey, that the driver had never had the remotest intention of taking me to the airport, and that we had now arrived at some completely different destination.

It was not so. Panic had made me open my eyes and I saw at once that we were still on the road. Moreover, the cars ahead and on either side were also stationary. Simultaneously, my eye lighted on some familiar shapes away over to the left and I realised that we were at Rungi. The knowledge brought some comfort, for Robin had pointed it out on a previous journey, explaining that these new buildings now housed Les Halles, which had been moved out from the centre of Paris. For a brief spell, I was able to convince myself that there must be dozens of lorries continually leaving and joining the road at this junction, which could easily account for the hold-up.

Unfortunately for my peace of mind, this rational view was not shared by my fellow motorists. Like an orchestra tuning up, tentative at first, then growing full-throated and confident, their horns went into action. In a few seconds the hideous blare was all around us. As though this were not enough, a new instrument could soon be heard to join in. Faint and faraway, from the back of the orchestra came the mournful bleat of sirens. Gradually, the volume increased, blotting out all other noise, and two police cars followed by an ambulance went careering past on the wrong side of the road, headlights blazing, to warn the oncoming traffic.

I turned my head away and peered down at my watch. Forty minutes had passed since leaving the flat. Even if an advance were to begin immediately, we could not reach the air terminal in under twenty minutes behind schedule.

A secondary torment was the atmosphere inside the car, for we were in open country, with no shade, and my fur coat was like a dead weight with hot wires running through it. Just as once before, in Adela's drawing-room, I became overpowered by a mounting suffocation. But this time terror was the principal element and, with such strength as still remained to me, I willed myself to believe that Ellen and her captors were somewhere in this queue, perhaps even in the car in front or behind. The alternative, too dreadful to contemplate, was that they had driven to Orly from another direction, were already waiting and watching for my arrival and would never know how meticulously I had striven to keep my side of the bargain.

Five or six minutes went by in this fashion and then there came a small reprieve. Up to this point the driver had appeared to take no interest whatever in the proceedings, showing neither dismay at our situation nor curiosity as to the cause of it. I assumed that he was too stupid even for that. When the traffic moved he moved with it, and when it stopped he stopped, and that was the beginning and end of it. However, this was not the prevailing attitude, as I could tell horn the raised voices and slamming of doors. One man, perhaps in search of a fresh audience to complain to, came up and tapped on my driver's window. For a moment I thought he would ignore it; then, to my intense relief, he wound down the window and gave an enquiring grunt.

The immediate effect was to freshen the stifling atmosphere and the draught of clean air so far revived me that I was able to pay attention to the stranger's harangue. He spoke too fast for me, using unfamiliar words, but nevertheless I could pick up the gist of it. Some items were predictable, others less so. The cause of the delay, for instance, was an accident involving several vehicles, but whereas I had pictured the line of stationary traffic as stretching ahead to eternity, it transpired that we were not more than fifty metres from the scene of disaster. I also learnt that the accident had been brought about by some young hooligans in a diplomatic car overtaking a lorry at the same moment as its driver had also moved out to pass another car, with a trailer attached. No one, I gathered, had been killed, but the destruction was indescribable and many were gravely wounded. So far as I could follow it, our messenger then had some stem observations to deliver on the subject of the arrogance of commercial drivers and the iniquitous laws which allowed the sons and daughters of embassy officials to drive around the country like maniacs; but he had hardly got into his stride before he was brusquely interrupted. There was a sudden flurry of activity all around us and my driver ground the car into gear and lurched forward, without even pausing to wind up the window. Our visitor looked wildly around, with an aghast expression on his face, then shot off down the road to his own car.

We were on the move at last, inching forward in spasmodic bursts, but I no longer cared. Ten minutes earlier I had been convinced that I had touched the depths of despair, but there was still another layer at the bottom of the barrel.

Even before our informant was so rudely cut off, I had been visited by a premonition far more terrifying than anything which had gone before. The longer my imagination dwelt on that carnage we were now creeping up on and on the mutilated human beings being loaded on to the ambulance, the stronger grew my certainty that I knew who two of them were. Had it not been for the succession of jerks which accompanied this train of thought and which kept shaking me back into awareness, I think I might have fainted. Coinciding with the fifth or sixth of these punctuation points, there was yet another diversion, on an even more dramatic scale. I heard a shout of anger from the front seat, and the nearside passenger door swung open. I caught a blur of green and red tartan and heard a perky voice say:

'Okay, Tessa, you can sit up now. The operation's over.'

So I did as I was told and when my eyes had taken in the full glory of the scene I decided to postpone the fainting for a bit.

Ellen's face, a little pinched and pale, but smiling valiantly, was all in one piece under the check cap, and Jonathan had both arms inside the driver's window and wrapped around the steering wheel. I flung him the cushion, which he caught one-handed and pressed into the driver's face.

'That's the stuff,' I said. 'Stay here for a few minutes and keep him quiet. Ellen, you come with me. I'll need all the help I can get, but we're going to talk those policemen into getting a call through to the flat, if it's the last thing we do. If Robin goes into action now, he can catch those fiends before they get away.'

'I TOLD as many lies as I could think of,' Ellen said modestly. 'I thought it might help if I got things a bit mixed up.'

'They were that all right,' I assured her.

'You've all been so tricky and clever,' my agent sighed. 'Unlike me. If I hadn't been waiting for this call from California about a deal I'm putting through, I'd have remembered Tessa's boring old appendix and realised you were in some kind of a jam.'

'It was all for the best,' I told her.

'I wonder you should say such a thing,' Toby remarked sadly. 'I never saw anyone who looked more in need of medical attention than you do. It's not surprising. Going abroad invariably ends in this kind of disaster. Let it be a warning to you.'

'Well, it won't be. It was that hair-raising drive which temporarily knocked me out, plus the ghastly premonition about Ellen and Jonathan being the young couple in the crash. But I shall be as sound as a bell in the morning, and Heigh-ho, Heigh-ho it's off to work I go.'

Using my agent as intermediary, we had managed to waylay Toby practically as he stepped ashore and he had broken the rule of a lifetime by loading himself on to the evening plane. For some reason not precisely defined, my agent had chosen to accompany him. Whether her mission was to minister to his heart attack when the wheels left the ground or merely to jump on the band wagon was uncertain. Her own explanation was that she feared I might have a little difficulty in putting things right with the film studios and had nobly dropped all her urgent business in London to be on hand. However, I had long ago ceased to believe

188 | ANNE MORICE

a word she said and guessed that, whatever the reason, it was not that.

Lest there be any hint of churlishness in the foregoing, I should add that we were all delighted to see her. Having worked ourselves into the ground, going over and over the events of the past two days, it was like an injection of concentrated vitamins to begin again with a fresh audience.

Naturally, we had started by giving the floor to Ellen, the abducted heroine, but so far she had been unusually reticent and this was the first mild little boast we had heard from her. Perhaps she realised that by enlarging on the horrors of her capture and incarceration in the stables at Assy-les-Cygnes she would sooner or later provoke Toby into pointing out that she would have been better off with Miss Hacker, after all. Respecting her motives, I offered the stage to Jonathan:

'It was brilliant of you to think of looking for her there,' I told him. 'However did you hit on it?'

'Just logical thinking, I guess,' he replied, meaning it.

'He'd stayed there, himself, you see,' Ellen explained, more forthcoming on his behalf than her own. 'At least, not in the foul bit I was in, but where it was half converted. So he knew all the ropes.'

'Which is why he ran away from us on Sunday?' Toby suggested. 'He didn't fancy being rounded up by his mother and forced to spend another night in the straw?'

'He wasn't in the room when we made the plan about lunching at Assy, you see. It came as a bit of a shock to find himself on the Müllers' doorstep.'

It was all too easy to talk about Jonathan as though he had temporarily gone to the moon and I noticed that we had all slipped into the habit. Making a feeble effort to curb it, I said: 'Anyway, I forgive you for stealing the money. Naturally, if you were going to borrow your mother's car and drive through the dawn to Assy and then the airport, you needed every penny. In fact, I applaud it as a fine example of logical thinking.'

'We didn't dare come back to the flat, you see,' Ellen said. 'We guessed they'd be watching it.'

'Who's they?' Toby asked me.

'Her and her spy friend, of course. He was the real one. The other poor wretch was just a blind.'

'The other poor wretch being Sven?'

I glanced at Jonathan to see how he was taking this, but his reactions had reverted to the totally negative. So I turned back to Toby: 'That's right. She used Sven as a cover, but all the time she was running this affair with a man at one of the Iron Curtain embassies, and shooting around wherever she pleased in her sporty old C.D. car. Poor Sven, she deceived him on every level, even to trying to get him nailed for murder.'

'I guess he had it coming to him,' Jonathan said bitterly. 'He's such a puffed-up, darned old fool.'

Robin said thoughtfully: 'I wouldn't dismiss him quite so contemptuously. We all know what you think of your step-father, but he's not quite a fool, and he was certainly noble. When he got into real trouble his first thought was to protect his true love. And we should remember that she was his true love, from way back, long before he met your mother.'

'He was quite clever, too, in a funny way,' I admitted, 'in so far as there was usually method in his madness. Take that business with the script. It was such a crazy scheme, but it did achieve its object.'

'What script?' my agent asked, sitting up and taking considerably more notice.

'The one he was so keen to foist on me that he went to the lengths of pinching my suitcase and hiding it in the consigne. It was clever old Ellen who worked that out,' I said, smiling at her, but she still refused to be drawn.

'You said that he achieved his object,' Toby remarked, 'but you didn't tell us what it was.'

'There were two, and one was to foster the acquaintance. He was the world's most dedicated name-dropper, for a start, and no scalp was too small or obscure to add to the collection. The other was to ensure that I read this script he was so proud of. At first, Robin and I couldn't make out which of us was the attraction. When he cut me dead in the cinema, we concluded it must be Robin, but then I remembered an incident at Heathrow, when we were waiting for our plane, and the significance of it suddenly hit me.'

'Bring out your sledge-hammer,' Toby said, 'and let the significance of it suddenly hit us.'

'I should tell you that he had pretended not to know who I was, or that I had anything to do with the movies.'

My agent gave a gasp of incredulity, or at any rate a gasp, and Robin said:

'This has been nagging at Tessa for days. I swear it's what induced her to embroil herself in the case. Would you ever believe she could be so petty?'

'I'm not petty about not being recognised,' I protested, 'only about being recognised one minute and forgotten again the next.'

'I should think we all might be,' Toby said indignantly. 'Is that what he did? The filthy swine!'

'He really did. I daresay you've forgotten this, Robin, or didn't notice it, but when you first introduced us you said to him wasn't it funny how I'd been so convinced he had something to do with show business?'

'Vaguely, I remember.'

'Well, it made a much greater impact on him. He was so thrilled that he temporarily forgot himself and said something about, coming from me, he took it as a big compliment.'

'Did he? I don't remember that.'

'It is the kind of tribute which the recipient is likely to remember longer than anyone else,' Toby reminded him, 'so we had better take her word for it.'

'I'll make it easier for you by explaining that it was not I, personally, who counted. Anyone in my world would have done equally well. Anyway, having said it, he instantly realised his mistake, and to cover up he coyly asked me if I was going to Paris to do some modelling. Now, I ask you! If he really thought I might be a model, not even a well-known one, why should he be so bucked about my taking him for a script writer?'

'Because he's screwy, that's why,' Jonathan said, making one of his rare contributions.

'Wrong,' I said haughtily. 'There is a subtler explanation. The answer is that he did recognise me, straight off, when we were all queuing up at the check-in desk. I can't say when he decided to use the knowledge for his own ends, but my guess is that it was when he heard our plane would be late. That's when he made a beeline for Robin. Ellen and I were powdering our noses at the time, so it was the ideal set-up for him.'

'Why was it?' Toby demanded. 'Why not just stumble up to you and say: "Oh, Miss Crichton, I've admired you all my life and you're so very, very wonderful." That usually breaks the ice, in my experience.'

'Because the pretence of not knowing I was an actress was an essential part of the plan. His object was to get me to read his script and he realised that it was far more likely to succeed if everything appeared to happen by chance, without any design at all.'

'Was the script any good?' asked my agent, who has got where she has by cultivating a one-track mind.

'Not very,' I replied, 'but he was obviously convinced that it was a work of genius and would be a smash hit, if only he could get the right people to read it. The point is that he was shrewd enough to know that a lot of people use the approach which Toby has just described and immediately follow it by saying it's a funny thing, but they happen to have written a little something themselves, which they'd love to have your opinion about.'

'Yes, there has been some of that in my life, too,' he admitted.

'So you probably know as well as I do what comes next? You put on a fatuous grin and mumble something about being a bit tied up at present, but it doesn't deter them for an instant. By the very next post along comes a ton of manuscript, with a polite little reminder, and sometimes you dutifully wade through a few pages and sometimes you don't; and after a decent interval you post it back, with a little note of your own, to the effect that it's absolutely brilliant, etcetera, but perhaps a little more time should be spent on mastering the technical side, etcetera.'

'Why are you telling me all this?' he grumbled. 'If you think I know it already?'

'Simply because it is one of those hazards of life to which people like Sven are peculiarly prone. I bet he'd tried the formula half a dozen times and got exactly the same brush-off. However, being incurably optimistic, self-deluding and conceited, he had convinced himself that it was not the script that was at fault, but the attitude of the people who had been bludgeoned into reading it. And, let's face it, there could be a grain of truth in that.'

'He could have sent it to me,' my agent said. 'I'd have read it like a shot. Or got one of the girls to.'

'I expect he has sent it to you,' I retorted. 'I should never be surprised if there were a copy mouldering away at this very minute among those dusty old piles in your office. Anyway, when he learnt that you'd given me some scripts, he saw his opportunity and decided to insert his own among them. It was a trick which appealed to his devious mind and he could at least be sure that any prejudices I might start with would all be in his favour.'

'Very crazy,' Robin said. 'And afterwards, I suppose he had to steal our keys, so that he could pop in from time to time and see how far you'd got with it?'

I laughed: 'No, I don't think he was as sneaky as all that. I'm almost sure the keys fell out of your pocket by accident, but I daresay that when he went back to fetch the macintosh and found them on the floor the temptation was irresistible. Pêche said that he was out at a meeting that afternoon, but if he was I wouldn't mind betting that he called at a lock-smith on his way.'

'That's rather a fine distinction, and personally I would call it as near stealing as makes no difference. On the other hand, we could be doing him an injustice. We have no proof that he even handled the keys.'

'Oh yes, we have,' I replied. 'Or as near proof as makes no difference, to coin one of your phrases. I'm sure he had duplicates made and later on, when it became essential to get the script back, I think he used them. Not he, person-ally, because he was in prison by then, but he gave them to old Pêche, with clear instructions as to what she was to look for. That's when she took to haunting the café opposite.'

'Waiting and watching until everyone was out and she could nip upstairs and let herself into the flat?'

'Exactly; and I think she tried it, but of course you'd had the locks changed. So then she must have gone into conference with Sven and they hatched another plot. She came to us with a pathetic little tale about his languishing in jail with nothing to read. Frightfully feeble, really, because apart from their own bookshelves being crammed with stuff, you can buy all the English books you want in Paris. So when that didn't work she tried two more dodges. I left her alone in my bedroom and she went snooping through the desk to see if she could find the script there. As it happened, Ellen had borrowed it, as I very well knew, so that was a washout, too. As a last resort, she told me that Sven really needed some scenarios, so that he could copy the technique. In fact, she absolutely played into my hands and gave the show away completely.'

'Excuse me,' my agent said plaintively, 'but I'm not sure I follow this. Why, after all this trouble, was he so stuck on getting it back?'

'I wasn't sure that I followed it, either,' Toby admitted, 'though, thank goodness, I wasn't the one to say so.'

'It was the crux,' I told them. 'There is no other word for it. The script carried a full description of how Mrs Baker was murdered; written, I need hardly add, months in advance.'

'What you might call a dead give-away?'

'Yes, although I soon realised that if it was his own skin he was worried about, he'd have owned up about being in the cinema that night. I knew he was there and had heard his named called, however much they kept telling me it was impossible. So I guessed he was shielding someone else; and who but the real murderer?'

'And why should he want to do that?'

'Because he was dotty about her; and there's a pun there, for those of us who are sharp enough to see it.'

My agent looked rather put out, but after a while Toby said,

'A terrible one. You mean Dotty, short for Dorothea?'

'Alias Thea, alias Delphine. All those characters were very thinly disguised. Felix Marcus was the maniac doctor, and the hero was called Simon Charrington. Did you notice that, Ellen?'

She nodded, but still did not speak.

'So, having grasped that he was doing his Sydney Carton act and taking another's place at the guillotine, it only remained to discover who.'

'A mere bagatelle?'

'A process of elimination, to put it grandly. Naturally, I considered Adela first. Although the idea of her being a murderess was quite ludicrous,' I added hastily, for Jonathan's benefit. 'Then there was old Pêche, but she seemed rather an improbable person to be laying down one's life for. Also I doubt if she'd read the script. I'm certain she didn't type it because it was so untidily done, which is not her style at all. Probably he typed it himself. I expect that's what he was up to half the time, when he gave it out that he was working late on reports. So then I took another look at Thea. In some ways, she was the likeliest candidate of all; a proper femme fatale type and, allowing for the fact that he went through life in rose-coloured blinkers, she was a logical Delphine. Unfortunately, Robin and I had ruled her out.'

'How fascinating! Do tell us how you came to rule her in again.'

'It was Tessa's finest hour,' Robin said, 'and, paradoxically, the one she is least willing to talk about.'

'Paradox is the word. I can hardly credit it.'

'It was hard to accept, after all the struggle, that I didn't know as much French as I thought,' I said. 'Or to be precise, what a lot of words there are which sound roughly the same in both languages but have different meanings. Madame Stéfane was a great one for that. When she was stumped for an English word she just used a French one and anglicised the pronunciation a bit. For instance, she said ignore, when she meant "not knowing", and there was a much more vital slip which sailed right over me.'

Toby and my agent were watching me with suitably riveted expressions, so I paused long enough to give it the maximum effect, before saying:

'She translated "bague" into bag. It was such a trivial mistake, but it confused everything. You see, the reason for dismissing old Thea was that I'd got this entirely false impression that she'd walked through the Champ de Mars without any kind of bag. So, by only slightly bending the truth about the time of her arrival at IDEAS, she would have had the opportunity, but it was still inconceivable that she could have had the weapon. She would not only have to carry a whacking great spanner to the scene of the crime, where we now know she had a rendezvous with Leila Baker; she had then to use it for bloody murder and carry it quite openly all the way to IDEAS, so as to dump it in the basement car park. But of course it wasn't like that at all. The missing article was her ring, her "bague", if you prefer. I suppose she'd taken it off for a manicure or something, or maybe she made up the whole story about mislaying it, in order to impress on everyone what time she left the shop, in case the need arose. But I've got into the habit now of translating everything as I go along. The other day I was sitting in a café and I noticed the waiter was wearing a flashy great signet ring. That's when the truth began to dawn, and just to ram it home he reminded me, as I was leaving, that my sac was ouvert.'

'But she surely wouldn't have wished the time of her leaving the shop to be remembered?' Toby asked. 'Wouldn't it have been wiser to pretend that she left later than she did and hope to get away with it?'

'You'd think so, wouldn't you, but it was the other way round. The first part of her alibi had to be accurate, so that she could fake the second part. That's when she's sitting demurely in the hall at IDEAS, waiting for her husband to come down. The time is now ten to eight and the lift door opens, but instead of her husband out steps Sven. At least, that was her story, but of course it was pure fabrication. At a quarter to eight she was down in the basement, impersonating him, in the knowledge that he was already safely on his way to meet her at the cinema. It was her bad luck that Ellen and I picked the same film. I think I can safely say.' I concluded smugly, 'that, but for that unlucky accident, she would have got away with it.'

'Although this male impersonation act must have carried a certain risk?'

'Not so much as you might think. She and Sven are about the same height, for one thing, and Robin had already pointed out two other circumstances in her favour. One was the basement being so dimly lit and the other that, superficially, he was awfully easy to imitate. She could have fooled anyone at twenty yards, provided she'd had the forethought to put his hat and overcoat in the boot of her car. I expect he had more than one of those terrible outfits. In fact, I'd meant to check on that very point with Adela, but then Ellen got herself kidnapped and there were other matters to be dealt with.'

198 | ANNE MORICE

'She was pretty sure of herself, wasn't she?' my agent remarked critically. 'And of her loved one, too. What made her so confident he'd keep his silly mouth shut?'

'I've told you one reason, but she hadn't left him much choice, had she? All he could say was that she was the only single individual who'd read his script and therefore only she would have used that particular method of murdering someone. But it still wouldn't preclude his having done it, himself, and she only had to deny having read it. In the meantime, she'd practically pickled him in brine by contriving to get him in two places at once, believing that he could never prove that the cinema was the true one. That was what made her so scared of me, specially after she'd seen us walking down the road when she was shopping in Assy-les-Cygnes last Sunday with Adela. But the first and greatest risk was her poor old husband. I think it was when the police started raking up the past history of his T.B. clinic that she became afraid of his giving something away which would uncover what really happened there. So she ran up a fake suicide note and gave him a strong dose in his bedtime drink. Being a nurse, she'd have known exactly the right mixture. You may be interested to know that I got the idea of her being a nurse a long, long while ago. It was when I was bitten by the poodle and she made such a neat job of binding me up. You never saw anything so professional. When I read "The Waiting Room", that bit fell into place, too.'

'And what was her place?' Toby asked. 'I think that may well be my last question.'

'The place of one who loved money and would do anything to get it, including espionage. Here was a patient in that hospital, a young man who was due to die of his illness, so she may have been a bit careless where he was concerned, blithely believing that any secrets he may have unearthed would shortly be carried with him to the grave. However, against all the odds, he recovered and was about to be discharged. Naturally, she couldn't have that, so he got his in the hot milk, too. It was written off as criminal negligence and Dr Müller took full responsibility, but we'll never know whether he suspected her or not; probably not, since he married her when he came out of jail. Sven's first wife was a patient, too, and that's how he met and fell for Dorothea/Delphine.'

'I can't help it,' my agent said, 'I know one ought to let Toby have the last question, but why did Dorothea/Delphine want to murder this Baker woman?'

'And Robin shall have the last answer,' I said, bowing to him graciously.

'Has he been holding out on us?'

'Not at all,' Robin replied, 'I've been involved on the fringes of that part of the affair which concerned the leakage of information; and that, of course, is what eventually led to the murder.'

'Indeed? You mean this Baker lady was working for the counterspy brigade?'

'No, on the contrary, she had nothing whatever to do with it, as I could have told Thea Müller, if she'd taken the trouble to ask me. Unfortunately, she followed her own instinct, which let her down quite badly. I admit she had some excuse. The Bakers had switched around from country to country for the last few years and their last posting was in London, where Thea and her chum also had their contact. It may have been this which first gave her the idea that Leila Baker was something a little more threatening than just an innocent member of the personnel department, but also the poor woman had acquired quite a reputation for poking her nose into other people's business and generally making a nuisance of herself. Thea, who had quite a load on her conscience, put two and two together and made sixteen out of it. In other words, she came up with the answer that Mrs Baker had been planted at IDEAS for the specific purpose of nosing out the spies and was getting dangerously near to doing so. It was a very stupid mistake.'

'And a very nasty one, too, in my opinion.'

'But one has to remember that it wasn't the first murder she'd committed, and it wasn't to be the last. I suppose that killing the people who got in her way had become a natural reaction. In fact, Tessa and Ellen have a theory that it wasn't the first go she'd had at Mrs Baker. It seems that the old sitar player drank down the contents of her carafe five minutes before he dropped dead, so that may have had a dose in it, too. There's no way of proving it, but Thea could well have been in the vicinity on the night of the concert. There was so much confusion and so many people milling around that one more or less wouldn't have stood out. Also she could have got into the hall from the other entrance before the proceedings even started. Her husband was working over at the main building at the time, so she had a perfect excuse if anyone had chanced to notice her. I don't expect we'll ever know the truth about that.'

'It seems to me that we know quite enough already to form rather a low opinion of her,' Toby remarked. 'It is shattering to recall that she once had Ellen in her clutches, however briefly. I suppose I shall have to be a terribly kind and indulgent father for the next ten years, to make up for it.'

EPILOGUE

'IT WASN'T quite fair, you know,' Ellen said reprovingly, winding her hair into a knot and tucking it inside the check cap.

'What wasn't?'

'All that stuff about a ring being une bague and a bag being un sac. You'd need to know heaps of French to get the hang of it. Now, if it had been Spanish . . .'

'You'd have caught on in a trice; I know. But there were lots of other signs to show which way the wind blew, and anyway there are things I am far less proud of than that.'

In a sense, we were back where we came in, for this conversation took place in the cloakroom at Orly. My producers, having learnt all and forgiven all, had gallantly suggested my taking a few days holiday, to recover from the atrocious ordeals. To be frank, I think they hoped to gain on the roundabouts of publicity what they lost on the swings of working days, but I had gratefully accepted the offer and we were all on our way to London. Jonathan had taken a fancy to explore the King's Road, and was also among the party.

'Which?' Ellen asked. 'Which things aren't you proud of?'

'Well, underestimating Jonathan, for one. It was absolutely heroic, the way he handled your rescue. And staging that motor accident with neither of you getting a scratch was a sheer marvel. Tears come into my eyes whenever I think of it.'

'Do they really?'

'Yes, they do. That's mainly why Robin and I have been tumbling over ourselves not to say nasty things about his old mum. And I take it all back about his being such a liar. I'm quite prepared to believe that his father has ice dispensers in every last Cadillac.'

Ellen had gripped the wash-basin with both hands and was rocking back and forth, as though in extreme agony.

Alarm changed to injured pride when I saw that she was laughing.

'Oh, you are funny, Tess. No wonder Robin gets so mad sometimes.'

'He doesn't get mad at all. Allow me to tell you . . .'

'Yes, he does, and it's not surprising. You will keep dashing from one extreme to the other. Just because Jono did one thing quite well, you have to go and make him into a saint; but it's not true about him having his own sports car, you know. The only driving he's ever done is in the field next to their house. He hasn't even got a licence.'

'Are you sure of that, Ellen? Then how . . . ?'

'The accident wasn't planned, it just happened. You see, we were in a bit of a hurry to get to the airport before you did.'

'Oh really? But, listen, won't he get into awful trouble?'

'Yes, of course he will,' she said, doubling up with mirth again. 'That's why he has this sudden urge to come to London. Luckily, no one was badly hurt, even though it was such a shambles. He's hoping that when they take everything else into consideration too, they'll cool off and only make him pay quite a small fine.'

'Well, of all the . . .' I began, and was cut short by a voice on the loudspeaker. It announced a delay of approximately twenty minutes in the departure of Air France flight Eight One Two, due to adverse weather conditions in merry old England.

'Here we go, then!' Ellen said. 'Now, I wonder who's going to get murdered on this trip?'

'You will,' I said mechanically, collecting my bague and sac and following her to the door, 'if you don't kindly stop . . .'

THE END

FELICITY SHAW

THE detective novels of Anne Morice seem rather to reflect the actual life and background of the author, whose full married name was Felicity Anne Morice Worthington Shaw. Felicity was born in the county of Kent on February 18, 1916, one of four daughters of Harry Edward Worthington, a well-loved village doctor, and his pretty young wife, Muriel Rose Morice. Seemingly this is an unexceptional provenance for an English mystery writer—yet in fact Felicity's complicated ancestry was like something out of a classic English mystery, with several cases of children born on the wrong side of the blanket to prominent sires and their humbly born paramours. Her mother Muriel Rose was the natural daughter of dressmaker Rebecca Garnett Gould and Charles John Morice, a Harrow graduate and footballer who played in the 1872 England/Scotland match. Doffing his football kit after this triumph, Charles became a stockbroker like his father, his brothers and his nephew Percy John de Paravicini, son of Baron James Prior de Paravicini and Charles' only surviving sister, Valentina Antoinette Sampayo Morice. (Of Scottish mercantile origin, the Morices had extensive Portuguese business connections.) Charles also found time, when not playing the fields of sport or commerce, to father a pair of out-of-wedlock children with a coachman's daughter, Clementina Frances Turvey, whom he would later marry.

Her mother having passed away when she was only four years old, Muriel Rose was raised by her half-sister Kitty, who had wed a commercial traveler, at the village of Birchington-on-Sea, Kent, near the city of Margate. There she met kindly local doctor Harry Worthington when he treated her during a local measles outbreak. The case of measles led to marriage between the physician and his patient, with the couple wedding in 1904, when Harry was thirty-six and Muriel Rose but twenty-two. Together Harry and Muriel Rose had a daughter, Elizabeth, in 1906. However Muriel Rose's three later daughters—Angela, Felicity and Yvonne—were fathered by another man, London playwright Frederick Leonard Lonsdale, the author of such popular stage works (many of them adapted as films) as *On Approval* and *The Last of Mrs. Cheyney* as well as being the most steady of Muriel Rose's many lovers.

Unfortunately for Muriel Rose, Lonsdale's interest in her evaporated as his stage success mounted. The playwright proposed pensioning off his discarded mistress with an annual stipend of one hundred pounds apiece for each of his natural daughters, provided that he and Muriel Rose never met again. The offer was accepted, although Muriel Rose, a woman of golden flights and fancies who romantically went by the name Lucy Glitters (she told her daughters that her father had christened her with this appellation on account of his having won a bet on a horse by that name on the day she was born), never got over the rejection. Meanwhile, "poor Dr. Worthington" as he was now known, had come down with Parkinson's Disease and he was packed off with a nurse to a cottage while "Lucy Glitters," now in straitened financial circumstances by her standards, moved with her daughters to a maisonette above a cake shop in Belgravia, London, in a bid to get the girls established. Felicity's older sister Angela went into acting for a profession, and her mother's theatrical ambition for her daughter is said to have been the inspiration for Noel Coward's amusingly imploring 1935 hit song "Don't Put Your Daughter on the Stage, Mrs. Worthington." Angela's greatest contribution to the cause of thespianism by far came when she married actor and theatrical agent Robin Fox, with whom she produced England's Fox acting dynasty, including her sons Edward and James and grandchildren Laurence, Jack, Emilia and Freddie.

Felicity meanwhile went to work in the office of the GPO Film Unit, a subdivision of the United Kingdom's General Post Office established in 1933 to produce documentary films. Her daughter Mary Premila Boseman has written that it was at the GPO Film Unit that the "pretty and fashionably slim" Felicity met documentarian Alexander Shaw—"good looking, strong featured, dark haired and with strange brown eyes between yellow and green"—and told herself "that's the man I'm going to marry," which she did. During the Thirties and Forties Alex produced and/or directed over a score of prestige documentaries, including *Tank Patrol*, *Our Country* (introduced by actor Burgess Meredith) and *Penicillin*. After World War Two Alex worked with the United Nations agencies UNESCO and UNRWA and he and Felicity and their three children resided in developing nations all around the world. Felicity's daughter Mary recalls that Felicity "set up house in most of these places adapting to each circumstance. Furniture and curtains and so on were made of local materials. . . . The only possession that followed us everywhere from England was the box of Christmas decorations, practically heirlooms, fragile and attractive and unbroken throughout. In Wad Medani in the Sudan they hung on a thorn bush and looked charming."

It was during these years that Felicity began writing fiction, eventually publishing two fine mainstream novels, *The Happy Exiles* (1956) and *Sun-Trap* (1958). The former novel, a lightly satirical comedy of manners about British and American expatriates in an unnamed British colony during the dying days of the Empire, received particularly good reviews and was published in both the United Kingdom and the United States, but after a nasty bout with malaria and the death, back in England, of her mother Lucy Glitters, Felicity put writing aside for more than a decade, until under her pseudonym Anne Morice, drawn from her two middle names, she successfully launched her Tessa Crichton mystery series in 1970. "From the royalties of these books," notes Mary Premila Boseman, "she was able to buy a house in Hambleden, near Henley-on-Thames; this was the first of our houses that wasn't rented." Felicity spent a great deal more time in the home country during the last two decades of her life, gardening and cooking for friends (though she herself when alone subsisted on a diet of black coffee and watercress) and industriously spinning her tales of genteel English murder in locales much like that in which she now resided. Sometimes she joined Alex in his overseas travels to different places, including Washington, D.C., which she wrote about with characteristic wryness in her 1977 detective novel *Murder with Mimicry* ("a nice lively book saturated with show business," pronounced the *New York Times Book Review*). Felicity Shaw lived a full life of richly varied experiences, which are rewardingly reflected in her books, the last of which was published posthumously in 1990, a year after her death at the age of seventy-three on May 18th, 1989.

Curtis Evans

Printed in Great Britain
by Amazon